the grave

the grave

james heneghan

FRANCES FOSTER BOOKS

FARRAR, STRAUS AND GIROUX

NEW YORK

Distributed in Canada by Douglas & McIntyre Ltd.
Printed in the United States of America
Designed by Filomena Tuosto
First edition, 2000
10 9 8 7 6 5 4 3 2 1

Library of Congress Cataloging-in-Publication Data
Heneghan, James, 1930–
    The grave / James Heneghan. — 1st ed.
        p. cm.
    Summary: Thirteen-year-old Tom, an unhappy foster child in Liverpool, falls into a massive open grave and is transported to Ireland in 1847, where he finds himself in the midst of the deadly potato famine.
    ISBN 0-374-32765-3
    1. Ireland—History—Famine, 1845–1852—Juvenile fiction. [1. Ireland—History—Famine, 1845–1852—Fiction. 2. Time travel—Fiction.
3. Foster home care—Fiction. 4. Liverpool (England)—Fiction.
5. England—Fiction.]   I. Title.
PZ7.H3865Gr   2000
[Fic]—dc21   99-27599

FOR MAUREEN

I owe a debt of gratitude to my editor, Frances Foster,

and my copy editor, Elaine Chubb,

for their confidence and perseverance.

the grave

... caught like an animal in a leg-hold trap

Basically, I'm a loner.

My name is Tom and I'm small for my age, which is thirteen and three-quarters. My mother left me crawling in Toys on the fifth floor of Lewis's department store when I was a baby and never came back for me. It was downtown Liverpool, Christmas, 1961. She probably kissed me on the cheek and told me, "Be a good boy," before she took off, but that's guesswork because how would I know that? Maybe she wished me a Merry Christmas. Anyway I never saw her again. They found a note pinned to me that said "Tommy." That was it, just "Tommy," no birth date, no second name, nothing. I don't even know whether she was sad or glad to be rid of me, but whenever I think of her I always imagine her saying, "Be a good boy, Tommy," and then taking the elevator down to the main floor and pushing her way through the revolving doors and running down Renshaw Street with her coat flapping.

I've been a loner ever since.

I still live in Liverpool, a few miles from Lewis's downtown, in a suburb called Old Swan, and I've got a story to tell. I'll be surprised if anyone believes it because sometimes I don't even believe it myself. But I've got to tell it.

It all started when I fell into the black hole.

Or was dragged, more like.

It wasn't one of those black holes way out in space, the kind that's supposed to suck up asteroids and space debris like a vacuum cleaner—no; this black hole was just a deep pit on a construction site, hidden behind a corrugated steel fence in the school yard. Men and machines had been working behind the high fence for a whole year, building the new school, though the actual building hadn't started yet because they were still working on the excavation. Why a whole year just to dig a hole? Nobody knew the answer. Rumors of all kinds were flying around: the delay was caused by the important discovery of ancient Roman ruins and the government had sent experts to check it out; or the workmen had uncovered the grisly remains of a singer, famous for her blond boldness and unconventional music, who disappeared a year ago and was now found murdered, chopped into pieces with a butcher knife; or the construction crew had discovered a hoard of buried treasure dating back to the Spanish Armada; or they had found a secret tunnel to Australia. Everyone laughed at the rumors but soon stopped when they saw fresh rolls of razor wire and a uniformed guard put on to patrol the fence perimeter twenty-four hours a day.

For several days I'd felt a powerful impulse to explore behind the fence, like there was something, or somebody, commanding me; like my very life depended on it. It was nothing but my overactive imagination, I told myself, the exciting idea of exploring Roman ruins more than a thousand years old, or of seeing Spanish gold, or of being the first through the tunnel to Australia.

I thought about it so hard I couldn't sleep.

When I slipped out of bed Brian heard me getting up and thought I was running out on him, so I ended up having to take him with me.

We crept out under the cover of moony darkness. Don't think I wasn't scared, because I was. I was scared out of my mind if you really want to know the truth. But I just had to see what was behind the fence, no matter what.

The moon was almost full, but dodgy with thin cloud. The urge was stronger the closer I got, like there was a magnet dragging me. We got to Snozzy's school yard—Snozzy's is what all the kids call St. Oswald's—and hid in the bushes near the church.

Brian was scared, too. "I don't like this place, Tom," he whined. "Could we go back now?"

"You can go back, but I've got to see what's behind the fence."

Brian said, "Wha?"

I should mention that Brian's bread isn't baked all the way through.

"Or you can stay here and wait for me," I told him.

"I'm scared, Tom. Don't leave me here by myself!"

"Then shut up."

The uniformed guard stood with his back to the fence smoking a ciggy. He finally ground the butt end under his boot and started patrolling slowly along the fence. When he disappeared round the bend I said, "Let's go!"

We moved sharpish, me pushing Brian along to keep him moving. The gap under the corrugated fence was wide enough to drive a double-decker bus through. We dived under and crouched on the inside, listening.

Not a sound. The moon edged out from behind thin cloud. I looked around quickly but there wasn't much to see, only an ordinary construction site: soil piled in high pyramids; a crane with a long jib; a forklift gleaming yellow in the moonlight; picks and shovels leaning against the church wall; a stack of timber; black shadows everywhere.

I could almost hear my heart hammering.

And again the pulling, like that black hole in space I already mentioned, trying to suck me into its dark belly.

We stood and edged forward.

Brian tripped. "Look out!" I grabbed his arm to stop him falling.

I stared down at the object Brian had tripped over. It was like, what, a thighbone? And then I saw boxes, several of them scattered about on the ground, plain wooden boxes, but coffin-shaped and horrible.

I kicked at the side of a box. The rotted wood collapsed easily. I kicked again, harder this time, and part of the top came away. I crouched and leaned forward, staring into the box. Rags and . . . bones. It was a coffin, sure enough. Terrified, I backed off, my chest pounding, and bumped into Brian. That scared me even more.

"I wanna go home," Brian moaned.

"Shurrup!" I said fiercely. "You wanted to come, didn't you?"

I moved on and Brian followed, moaning, clutching my jacket.

The rumors were wrong. All that secret digging behind the fence; it was really just an old graveyard. Nothing to be scared of in a graveyard, I told myself; dead people couldn't harm me.

The moon rode clear and I froze. One more step and we would have fallen into a black pit the size of a swimming pool. I grabbed Brian's arm so he wouldn't topple in and stood peering down into the black hole, Brian clutched to me and whimpering like a beaten dog.

In the silvery light I could see coffins, hundreds of them, in a pit more than twenty feet deep. This was way scarier than I'd expected. This was too much. I was finding it difficult to breathe. I wanted to run away but I was caught like an animal in a leg-hold trap.

Brian was pulling at me and crying at the same time. "Tom! Tom!"

I sucked in a deep breath to try and calm my bursting chest and found the smell from the open grave wasn't bad the way you'd expect from so many dead people, but was sweet and musty instead, like mushrooms, or like those tiny samples of extra-old cheese they give away in Sainsbury's on Saturday mornings. But it wasn't the smell that got to me, it was the feeling that something in the black pit was reaching out to me, pulling me, that same urge again, the one I'd been getting for the past couple of days, but stronger now and more powerful. It terrified me if you really want to know the truth.

"Do you feel anything?" I asked Brian, trying to keep my voice from shaking.

He pulled at me, crying and moaning. "I wanna go home, Tom!"

So did I. I tore myself away from the pit and its stacks of boxed skeletons and started back toward the fence, Brian still clutching my jacket, but something was dragging me back and it wasn't Brian. I struggled, but it was like trying to run in deep water.

"Hold it right there!" Bright beam of light in my face. The guard! I swore aloud, unable to see anything in the blinding light.

"Run for it, Brian!"

"Tom! Tom!" Brian screamed.

I moved. The next thing I knew I was falling into the black pit, and I didn't know if it was because Brian, moaning and terrified, had stumbled against me, or if it was something in the grave reaching out and grasping me and dragging me down, down, into its terrible darkness.

...a thousand red-hot needles

I dropped through darkness black as pitch, struggling for breath, with a tightness that felt like bony hands clamped around my chest. I was terrified. I screamed, long and loud. And then blacked out.

Dark nothingness.

So this was death.

Floating weightlessly, like an astronaut—

—a glimmer of green light, and a goblin of a thing—like those pictures you see in books of the devil, except I saw no tail—madly grinning, round eyes staring, holding aloft a lighted lantern to peer at me . . . raising his staff . . . and I was falling again, terrified . . . terrified . . .

I emerged from darkness into a foreign land, burning with pains.

Daylight, with no sign of a living soul, perched on a high cliff with the wind tearing at me, gulls screaming overhead, pains stitching my insides with a thousand red-hot needles. I howled. I cried. I clenched my teeth against the pains and rolled on the ground and beat my fists on the earth.

After minutes that seemed like hours, the pains started to diminish and I was able to look down at the sea roaring and pounding on black rocks hundreds of feet below. Behind me there was nothing but deserted moor, no trees, only green prickly stuff, gorse or heather, and above me a storm-black sky.

I was alive.

But the pains in my guts, combined with the lingering memory of the grinning goblin man with his staff and lantern, and the screams of seabirds wheeling and massing against the cliff face and over my head, still terrified me. I pushed myself back from the cliff edge and sat perfectly still, trying to get a grip on myself, trying not to panic. The pains calmed some more, and then after a while they went away.

I was alone, which was nothing new: loners are always alone.

I tried to figure it all out, starting with my clothes: jeans, T-shirt, old navy nylon jacket flapping in the high wind, gray socks that used to be white, old beat-up runners. Nothing much in my pockets except a few coins, a thick rubber band I used as a catapult to shoot spitballs and other stuff across the classroom, and a matchbox. I turned my back to the wind and opened the matchbox. Crouched inside was Michael Jackson, a nifty black beetle I'd saved from the wheels of a 14A at a Derby Lane bus stop like, what, a couple of days ago? I'd left him sleeping in the matchbox, along with bits of soil and leaves I'd shoved in so he wouldn't starve, though I wasn't sure what beetles ate, my *Science Facts* book being unhelpful on the subject. It had a section on black holes eating planets and stuff and mentioned black beetles but didn't say what they liked to eat. I'd put in a string of spaghetti left over from last night's supper, which tasted like boiled underwear as usual, planning to set him free in a juicy clump of grass as soon as I'd examined him under my magnifying glass. I prodded him, but he didn't move. I closed the matchbox and stuck it back in my pocket; Michael Jackson was in a state of shock, same as me.

But where was I?

I looked about me. Then I remembered Brian. And the coffins. And falling—or being dragged, because that was what it had felt like—into the grave, and that green light, and the goblin man with the staff . . . I felt my head. Seemed okay. I looked down at myself again: clothes and hands dirty from scrambling under the fence, jeans muddy at the knees. I got to my feet and stood facing the moor with the wind beating at my back.

The pains had gone but I tingled all over, like maybe I had

died and gone to some windy purgatory, with only crying birds and a black sky. I squinted around again as the wind tore at the gorse and at my hair, already stiff with salt from spray blown up from the base of the cliff. It was like no place I'd ever seen; there were no people, no ships on the sea, nothing but the cliff and the birds and the rocks below, and flat green countryside going on for miles, and a dark bulk of mountain way off in the distance.

My knees started to tremble.

I clenched my fists and gave myself a talking-to, the way I usually did whenever I felt scared, like all the times I had to start over at a new fozzy—foster home—and the other kids were staring at me like I was there to steal their comics, or like starting over at a new school, and after a while I felt not too bad.

But soon I was shivering from the cold, so I zipped my jacket up to the chin and hunched my shoulders and started walking along the edge of the cliff, not too close because the wind was strong enough to pick me up and hurl me over, and whenever I came to a curved part I took a shortcut through the gorse. I noticed I was on a descending path, so I kept going, staying on the path, while lightning flashed far out to sea and thunder rolled and grumbled. The rain started, a few heavy drops at first, then a steady pisser, and soon I was soaked through. Except for pins and needles in my fingertips, most of the tingly feeling had gone, extinguished by the heavy rain. I kept plodding through the storm, suddenly realizing that my feet seemed directed, like something was telling them which path to take. I felt scared again. I wasn't sure if this place was real. Could even be a different planet.

The path, rising now, veered away toward the mountain, looming higher and darker before me. I was sheltered from the wind a bit as the ground became more hilly, the gorse giving way to thin grass and bog, but the rain kept on, an aggressive, bullying kind of rain that boomed and hissed at me. Then I noticed a foul smell, something rotten, which reminded me of Brian's socks on the floor by his bed at night. Powerful bad whenever he forgot to take a bath, which was most of the time unless I reminded him. I looked around but couldn't see anything different, just the rain drumming on the ground.

I plowed on, letting my feet choose the way, shaking my head, feeling right sorry for myself, wet to the skin, shivering with the cold. I'd died and gone to hell. Smelled like hell when the wind of it came at you, the kind of pong that gets right up your nose.

The path, veering away from the mountain, now descended steeply toward a rocky cove, leaving the smell behind.

A bunch of people were gathered around a damaged boat and the body of a drowned, half-naked boy sprawled lifelessly over a smooth boulder, bent so his head hung down a foot or so above the sand.

As I arrived a girl came running down a path on the other side of the cove. "Tully!" she screamed, throwing herself on the drowned boy and clasping his head between her hands, trying to wake him. A woman and a big lump of a boy followed behind the girl. When the woman, obviously the mother, saw the drowned Tully lying spread out on the rock she let out a howl of grief that echoed the harsh commotion of seabirds wheeling overhead. The other boy, wailing and crying, clutched the mother's arm.

The waves pounded on the rocks and the shattered boat, and sent a spray over the small crowd of ragged-looking villagers, men and women, most of them barefoot, and a bunch of snotty-nosed kids and babies.

A tall woman, thin as a broomstick, with sunken cheeks and hollow eyes, dressed like the other women in a long, dark dress and black knitted shawl, wrapped her arms about the mother and held her, talking in a foreign language. Then she said in English, "The sea is draining out of him, Maggie, but his soul is fled. God rest him now, for there's nothing that mortal man can do."

A second, gap-toothed woman, dressed the same as the first, reached down and tried to lift the young girl by the shoulders. "Tully is gone, child," she said. "It's only the Almighty can help him now."

The girl ran to the mother and flung her arms about her.

"My heart is scalded this black day!" cried the mother, clasping the girl fiercely.

The men, thin and ragged, hats in their hands, stood with heads bowed; the women clung together, wailing or crying, and the whole thing looked pretty goofy to me, like except for folding the drowned boy over the rock, facedown, nobody

seemed to have tried any proper first aid. They needed someone to tell them what to do.

I yelled at the tall gaunt woman and the people clustered behind her, "Has anyone tried artificial respiration?"

"Fergus has sent for the priest," someone said. "Father
O'Dwyer should be here any minute."

I crouched beside the boy called Tully, trying to remember
my basic first-aid classes at Snozzy's, wishing now that I'd paid
more attention instead of fooling around so much. I felt for a
pulse in the neck, at the carrot artery. Nothing, not even a
tremor. Which meant I should try CPR, which a kid named
Willy Ardren said stood for Chest-Pushing Routine, and which
everyone in the class thought was funny, especially when another kid named Larry Ford said he wouldn't mind doing
some CPR on the student teacher, who was young and pretty,
with dimples and a generous amount of interesting-looking
chest.

The tide was coming up the strand almost as far as Tully's
dangling head. I yelled to one of the men, "Help me lay him
out on the sand." I grabbed the kid's feet and waited for the
man to lift the shoulders. "Hurry!" I yelled.

Two men sprang forward to help, lifting Tully, turning him
over, and plonking him down on the beach.

I kneeled beside the body and put my hand on the chest and
leaned my weight on it and started pushing. Up-down, up-
down, up-down, trying to remember how many pushes to do
before I had to breathe into the kid's cold cake-hole. I counted
ten pushes, then straightened his jaw so the tongue was free

and did a couple of breaths, and kept that up for about five minutes while the tide rushed in and swirled about my knees, hoping I was doing it right, while everyone watched, puzzled, wondering what I was up to. I could see out of the corner of my eye that each time I pinched his nose and gave him the old kiss of life, blowing air into him, they muttered and cackled at each other in a funny language like a flock of pigeons. One old biddy said to me, "Get up and leave him to the priest, boy." Another said, "It's a terrible sad thing, so it is." Another cried, "It's no wonder. Wasn't he fishing on a Sunday. On the holy Sabbath." A man told her, "Be quiet, woman!"

I glanced up one time and thought I saw in the crowd the goblin from my nightmare, leaning on his staff and watching me with a mad grin and round, mocking eyes, and when I tried to see more of him he'd gone.

One of the men said, "It's no use, boy. There isn't the breath of life in the lad. Can you not feel the cold stillness of him?" He bent and took me by the arm, trying to coax me away.

"Leave him be, Fergus!" yelled the girl angrily, pushing the man back and watching me intently.

Some of the women started wailing in high-pitched wolfy howls.

A woman said, "The sea is the devil." Then they all started talking and keening and wailing and asking God's mercy, calling on the angels and saints to help them in their troubles and forgive their sins, and a whole lot of other stuff you wouldn't want to know about. One of the men lifted the boat easily off the rocks and carried it up onto the beach, away from the tide.

I stopped the CPR for a few seconds and got the men to help me drag Tully out of the water, and then went back at it and felt real chuffed when finally I felt a flutter of pulse at the kid's neck and kept going, pushing and pinching and breathing into him, till the pulse got stronger, and then I kept at it some more until he was choking and breathing and dribbling seawater, and I knew he'd be okay and I was double-chuffed.

I rolled him over onto his front and thumped his back to get any more water up—I wasn't sure if I was supposed to do that—but after a bit, he finished choking and coughing and the girl, his sister, I guessed, knelt beside him, weeping for joy. Then she leaped up and threw her arms about me and cried, "Bless your heart! It was the good Lord sent you!" Hanging on my neck, feelings bursting out of her, half strangling me.

"It's a wonder!" cried the mother, making a sign of the cross and staring at her son.

The big lumpy kid, the girl's second brother, danced up and down making small whooping noises, then he launched himself at me and crushed me so hard to his chest in a slobbering bear hug that I gave a yell of pain.

"Brendan!" said the girl firmly, pulling at the boy's arm. "Stop that now."

Brendan released me. He was so like Brian—no resemblance in the facial features—but the same bulk and strength, the same dark head, the same piping, childish voice.

"It's a miracle!" said Fergus, looking up at the dark sky.

"A holy miracle!" cried the women.

"A saint in disguise!"

"May the heavens rain glory on your young head!"

"Holy Resurrection!"

As the mother wrapped her shawl about Tully's shivering shoulders she turned to me and cried, "God sent us a holy angel."

Now that Tully was recovered and sitting up, I could take a good look at him.

I gaped in astonishment.

I might have been looking in a mirror. Before me, battered by the storm, half-drowned, and shivering with the cold, was my double.

. . . a boy with my face

The boy called Tully looked exactly like me.

Like identical twins. Except Tully was older by a couple of years or so. The only other difference I could see was that, except for a brush of fringe that fell over his eyes, Tully's dark hair was short, cut unevenly, like he had cut it himself with a knife; my own hair was the usual 1974 mop, same as the other kids' at Snozzy's.

But he wore my face.

Or I wore his.

I had been studying him, but he hadn't looked at me yet, not properly; he was still kind of stunned. And so was I. I mean, "stunned" would be a mild word for what I felt; "blown away" might be more like it, or "annihilated" would be even better: here I was in the middle of nowhere and I meet my clone, my exact duplicate almost. The only possible explanation was that when I was dragged into the grave with the coffins I must've gone mad, and I was having visions and all this wasn't happening to me. I pinched my thigh, hard, and that seemed real enough, and the wet clothes sticking to me and the penetrating cold seemed real enough, too. So if it was all real, then I was in a place I'd never seen before, with a crowd of dippy strangers. If it wasn't real, then I was hallucinating, or lying dead of a broken neck in Snozzy's secret bone orchard, or something equally crazy, I didn't know what.

The rain turned to drizzle as the black sky retreated over the mountain. The second brother was still making little whoops of delight and thumping me approvingly on the back. The girl and her mother sighed and fussed over Tully as they helped him up the hill. Viewed from behind, Tully was taller than the mother and the girl, and a few inches taller than me—when you're short you notice other people's height more—and the loopy brother was bigger than everyone.

Like Brian.

We made our way along a cart track followed by the beach crowd. I didn't mention it because it's embarrassing, but if you really want to know the truth, all the time we were moving up the hill away from the cove the men were shyly shaking me by the hand, and the women touching me lightly with their fingers, then crossing themselves, like I was, who, Mahatma Gandhi? Mother Teresa? The kids at school would wet themselves laughing if they could see the look on my face.

I peered ahead into the drizzle and saw a cottage in the distance at the foot of the mountain, and then I could see another. The cart track led into a village made up of maybe a dozen small stone cottages or huts. It reminded me of Greek village pictures. Except the sky was gray instead of blue. Definitely not Greek. But not English either.

The cottages were made of uncemented stones, one dry stone piled or wedged on another, and the thatched roofs were held down against the wind with ropes and boulders. The village had an ancient look to it, like something you'd see in a history book, and it added to the craziness, making me feel like I was in someone else's dream.

A man was waiting anxiously, propping himself weakly against a wall. When he saw Tully he made a sign of the cross. "Is the curragh safe, boy?" he called, coughing.

Tully hung his head. "It will need the mending, Da."

"A pox on your curragh!" the mother said to Da angrily. "It's your son you ought to be asking about; wasn't he destroyed entirely, dead and drowned, but for the grace of God and His Blessed Mother and this brave young lad here, an angel sent by heaven to bring him back to us? Isn't that the truth, Fergus? Wasn't the lad just after laying his hands on Tully and bringing him back to life? Didn't he breathe on him like the Lord breathing life into the first clay of mankind?"

"It's as she says, right enough, Thaddy," Fergus said to the father. "If I hadn't seen it with my own two eyes I would never believe it."

The villagers stood around, listening to every word, nodding and sighing: ". . . our own two eyes . . . Holy Mother of God . . . back from the dead, right enough."

The mother and the girl were studying me. The girl stiffened and took a step back. Her puzzled gaze went to my hair and face, then fell to my jacket and jeans and shoes and back to my face, her eyes widening in alarm. "Ma! Will you look at him!"

"What is it, Hannah?" Ma looked at me and her mouth dropped open. "God save us!"

"Wha?" said Brendan.

He sure sounded like Brian.

"You're Tully's double!" Hannah said to me, her blue-gray eyes wide with astonishment.

About my own age or a bit younger, she was thin, with a dark brown head that came level with my eyes. She had a dark smudge on her white nose, and, like most of the villagers, was barefoot, and wore a black shawl over the shoulders of a faded blue cotton dress that came to her knees.

Captured by her eyes, I couldn't help staring at her.

"He's the spit and image!" said Ma.

Tully, reacting to his mother's "spit and image," now stared at me with eyes like light bulbs. "God save us!" he cried, echoing his mother, and stood goggling at me, his mouth hanging open in fear and astonishment.

The villagers' eyes moved from Tully's face to mine and back again. "Well I never!" said a woman. " 'Dentical twins," said another.

"Who are you?" asked Hannah.

I couldn't answer her. I wasn't sure who I was anymore if you really want to know the truth. If she called me Walt Disney I'd believe her.

Ma made a hurried sign of the cross. "Maybe it was the shee-og sent you and not the angels in heaven."

"The shee-og are the faeries," explained Hannah, seeing my bewilderment.

Small and thin with elfin eyes and cheekbones, she looked like a faery herself.

She spoke to her brother teasingly over her shoulder while looking mischievously at me. "The faeries it was who stole your face, Tully, and sent him to us."

"Tell me what happened below on the strand, Fergus," said the father.

Fergus told him.

A woman cried, "It was a miracle!"

The father wrapped his arms about his son and held him. "Tully, Tully," he groaned. "You should never have gone out. Didn't I tell you I could smell a storm coming."

"Get back into the bed, Thaddy," ordered Ma, "before you drop dead in the street."

"Ah, Maggie, leave me be! Didn't I almost lose a son this dark day!"

Tully, fearful and suspicious, was still staring at me, a rancid glitter in his blue eyes, like I *had* stolen his face. I could feel his dislike and hostility cutting through me like a knife.

Was that why the grave had dragged me to this strange place, to save the life of a boy with my face, a boy who seemed determined to make me his enemy?

4

... capturing my heart

I tore my eyes away from Tully and looked about me. Except for the small crowd of people the unpaved street was empty. There were no animals—cats, dogs, hens, pigs—and no cars or trucks or bikes. The village, like the landscape, had a clean, bare, windswept look to it. But then I caught a whiff of that foul smell from earlier and guessed it was coming from the rows of plants, most of their leaves blackened, growing in heaped furrows in terraces along the lower slopes of the mountain behind the cottages.

Tully shot me a final unfriendly look and followed his family into their cottage. Fergus and the others left.

I stood alone in the street.

Hannah ran out and took me by the hand. "Come in out of the rain."

I let her lead me inside.

I looked about me. With just two tiny window openings—no glass—the cottage was like a cave, with no furniture, only a few packing crates, one with papers on it and some mugs and plates. There were small wooden religious figures perched on wall stones. The floor was just plain dirt, packed and hard, with a shelf of slate or smooth stone near the fireplace. A lidded black pot hung over the fire from a chimney hook and two other pots of different sizes sat on the floor near the fire. I looked for a clock but couldn't see one. The papers on the packing crate seemed out of place in this poor hut, for there was no sign of other papers or books of any kind. I stole a glance: it was the kind of newssheet they give out at church on a Sunday. It had a title, like a newspaper: *Achill Missionary Herald* and was printed in English. In bold black letters at the top was the date: September 1847.

A dizziness came over me, like I'd just stumbled off a roller coaster.

It had to be a mistake.

The father lay down on his bed—not really a bed but a raised wooden platform supported by stones—while the mother sat on a packing crate and started poking at the fire with a stick.

The rain dripped off my wet clothes onto the dirt floor.

"What place is this?" I asked.

Hannah, misunderstanding my question, said, "The Monaghans'. I'm Hannah, and this is my ma and da and my brothers, Brendan and Tully."

Before I could ask anything more, Ma said, "Get out of your wet things, all of you. Hannah, bring the bits of blanket, will you? Brendan, go out and fetch some turf."

Hannah rummaged through a small pile of clothing in the corner and pulled out an armful of thin, ragged blankets. Tully, keeping his distance from me, took one and I took another. Brendan, happy to be useful, hurried outside to fetch whatever it was his mother had asked.

Hallucinating, that was it! 1847! The Mullen mind out of control.

The paper was a hundred and twenty-seven years old!

Tully turned his back as he peeled off what was left of his torn trousers. I saw his bare bum. Hannah took no notice of her naked brother. Brendan returned, still smiling happily, proud of his strength, arms overloaded with what looked to me like dried sods from the bog. He dropped them beside the fire and brushed off his hands on the back of his trousers. Tully wrapped the thin blanket about himself.

"Take off your things before you catch your death, boy," said Ma, fussing over me like I was one of her own.

Hannah grinned, her eyes alight with mischief, waiting to see me strip right there in front of everyone as Tully had done.

Embarrassed, I retreated to the darkest corner and turned my back and knotted the blanket about myself before struggling out of my wet things. Besides, I didn't want Hannah to see the heart-shaped birthmark I had on my bum—exactly like the one I'd just seen on Tully's backside: same size, same shape, same place.

Tully, talking to his sister, but his cold eyes on me, said, "Maybe you were right about the shee-og, Hannah. This young fellow has no name, and he's my living image. Perhaps he's here to take my place!"

"Give up your blathering, Tully," said Hannah. "He saved your miserable life this day down on the strand. The shee-og is nothing but silly superstition and right well you know it."

"It's only silly superstition when you say it is," said Tully angrily.

"Away with you! Mean and ungrateful! It's thankful you should be to the one who saved you," Hannah shouted at him.

Brendan's big silly grin disappeared and his eyes darted anxiously between his brother and sister.

"Stop it, you two," growled Ma.

Brendan relaxed.

The mischievous look returned to Hannah's eyes. She stuck out her tongue at Tully, then made a grab at my blanket like she was about to pull it off and leave me standing naked in front of them all, but she grabbed my shoes and clothes instead and spread them out on the floor in front of the fire to dry.

Ma threw a sod of turf on the fire, then signaled for me to sit near. I sat. The turf burned like coal, with a glowing red heat, and gave off a sweet smell, like pipe tobacco. Ma placed another thin blanket about my shoulders. Tully, silent and unfriendly, crouched near the fire and began whittling intently on a piece of wood. I tried to see what it was he was carving, but when he saw me looking he turned his back to me. Ma went to him and stood over him and gently pushed the fringe of hair from his eyes.

Hannah had been examining the heavy metal zipper on my nylon jacket, drying by the fire. "What kind of a yoke is this?"

I didn't answer. I couldn't. My head was spinning. I took the jacket, fastened the zip, and handed it back to her.

"I never saw the likes of it!" said Hannah. "Look, Ma!" She zipped and unzipped several times, demonstrating.

"Will you look at that!" said Ma, bringing the jacket close to her eyes like it was a string of pearls. Cautious, she didn't touch the zipper. "It's a thing of wonder right enough." She held it out to her son. "Will you take the look at that!"

The jacket was old because I'd had it a couple of years. I'd grown hardly at all; I was a stunted plant in need of a walloping good dose of fertilizer. I hoped they wouldn't notice I had a zip on the fly of my jeans.

Tully turned away, rejecting the jacket and fixing me with a look of naked dislike. "I'll not lay a finger on the work of the shee-og! I'd sooner shake hands with the Devil."

"You should give thanks to Almighty God, Tully," said Ma quietly, "that the boy was sent to us this day."

"Let me!" said Brendan, snatching the jacket from his mother's hands and sitting on the floor to play with the zip. But it wouldn't work for him. "Show me?" he asked Hannah. She showed him. Concentration forced his tongue out between his teeth and success lit up his face. Like Brian.

The father started a fit of coughing and Ma went to him with water drawn from a bucket.

Hannah's mouth puckered mischievously at me. "Do you remember yet who you are?"

"My name is Tom Mullen."

"How do you come to be here, Tom Mullen?" Curiosity bursting out of her.

I shook my head. "I don't know."

She laughed, delighted, like she had found an interesting puzzle to solve. "Then where are you from?"

"Liverpool."

"In England?" said Hannah. "You traveled the long way, so."

"Liverpool is the great distance," the mother said doubtfully, like she didn't believe me. "What brings you to holy Ireland?"

"Ireland!"

"Ireland right enough," Hannah said, delighted with the look of horror I must have worn on my face. "Where else would it be? You must be the dreadful eejit not to know that."

"Dreadful eejit," Brendan repeated.

"Eejit" was "idiot," I knew that much because some of the old geezers in Liverpool use the same word. What I wasn't sure of was my sanity. Was I going mad? I rubbed my eyes, hoping the five people and their stone hut would go away and I was back in Old Swan with Brian again. How could I be in Ireland? I looked about me wildly.

Nothing had changed.

"You're in the village of Slievemore," the mother said quietly, sympathetically, seeing my confusion. Then she added, "On Achill Island."

"In County Mayo," added Brendan, like he was repeating a lesson.

"How did you get here all the way from Liverpool?" asked Hannah. "Did you come in a ship to Westport?"

I asked desperately, "What year is this?" The paper had to be wrong.

"Ah! It's the memory gone," said Ma. "I knew an ould man in Dooagh who lost his memory. One day he was right as rain and the next—phwit!—he was an imbecile, couldn't remember his own name, God rest his poor soul. Did you lose your memory, so?"

"Answer me! What year?"

"It's eighteen forty-seven, of course," Hannah said, frightened by my outburst.

The mother said to the father on the bed, "A strange thing the memory, to forget the year like that. And what strange thing is it that makes him the image of our own son, I wonder?"

Hannah and the mother asked me more questions, but I didn't answer. I could hardly understand them anyway because of their way of speaking and because of the mix-up in my head.

Tully reminded his mother of the tricks of the shee-og. "Why does he not know what year it is? Believe nothing he says," he warned.

The mother shook her head. "Didn't he save your life this

day, Tully. If it was the shee-og, then it was one of their good tricks, not bad." She turned to me. "There's no knowing what the Little People will do. They're terrible tricky. Aren't they just as likely to save a life as to bring dreadful misfortune."

I thought of the grinning goblin.

"Dreadful misfortune is right," said Tully bitterly. "There's many the poor soul in this distressful country dying of starvation this very minute because of the withering curse the shee-og have put on the potatoes." He crossed himself and whispered a prayer.

The words "starvation" and "potatoes" nudged me like a hard elbow to the ribs, and I remembered the foul smell. "Curse?" I said.

"There's no curse," the father said. "Don't listen to them, they'd have you believing the shee-og run the world. The potatoes have the blight for the third year in a row. It's a disease, not a curse. The spuds are healthy one minute and blacker than the hobs of hell the next. A disease is what it is."

Ma said, "It's the work of the shee-og, right enough. What else could it be?" She turned to me again. "But if you listen to the Reverend Nangle, the Protestant minister above at the mission house, it's a scourge sent by God on all Catholics. If you listen to the priest it's a disease brought in by Protestants. But I know the work of the shee-og when I see it, right enough. Every spud in the country is black with it. For the poor there's nothing else. There's beggars going about eating ould cabbage leaves, and grass and nettles off the side of the road—Hannah darlin', wipe that dirt off your nose, why don't you?"

Hannah dipped a cloth in a pot by the fire and presented her small white face and the cloth to her mother, who wiped the spot clean with a light, affectionate scrub. I looked at them all more closely: they were thin but didn't seem to be starving or suffering in any way. Brendan certainly wasn't, the size of him.

"There's plenty of fish in the sea, Da," Brendan said brightly, repeating something he had probably heard many times.

"It's the sea that keeps us going, right enough," said the father to me, "with the occasional fish or seabird. But the fishing is hard." He coughed. "And the curragh is too light a craft for heavy weather. What with the winds driving you into the rocks, and the high cliffs like the devil's own trap, it's not worth your life to be out in it most of the year. And you cannot—didn't I tell Tully this morning"—a bout of coughing—"wait for the better weather."

"Rest, Thaddy," said Ma. "Save your strength or that terrible cough will be the undoing of you." She turned to me. "He's over the worst of it, thank God. He took the damp cold to his chest. Didn't we think at first it was the famine fever he had."

The father said to me, "Poor, starving people come to Achill for fish and bring the fever with them. I never saw times so hard. Now they're leaving Ireland by the thousands, making for England or America."

I was dizzy trying to understand them.

"Will we go to America, Da?" Hannah asked brightly.

"There'll be no talk of leaving," said the father. "The English will never stand by and see this country die of starvation."

"Ireland" and "potatoes" and "famine" rang bells in my

head, which only added to the queer feeling that I was in the wrong place at the wrong time. More and more I felt like I'd been handed a part in a school play and I didn't know my lines and everyone was anxiously waiting for me to speak.

And then a thought came that had nothing to do with my crazy predicament. The fire would bake Michael Jackson in his box! I pulled the blanket tight about my shoulders, slipped the matchbox from my jacket, still in Brendan's big hands, and went to the doorway. It was almost dark. The wind, blowing the smell of rot away from the cabin, smelled sharp and fresh. The muddy street was deserted, and the dark emptiness of the sky was like God had picked me up and put me in His match-box. I crouched down and tipped Michael Jackson into the weeds by the road, happy to see him crawling and free. I shook out the bits of spaghetti and other stuff, then went back inside and shoved the empty box back in the jacket pocket.

"Where will you go after here, Tom Mullen?" asked Hannah, kneeling at my feet and looking up at me, her small face creased with concentration.

"I don't know."

"D'you think maybe you would like to stay awhile?"

"I don't know," I said again, though if you want to know the truth I did and I didn't know. On the one hand, in spite of Tully's unfriendliness, I felt drawn to this family, had never felt such a warm sense of belonging, not since the Feinbergs, who I don't think I mentioned yet. On the other hand, I was scared of what was happening to me, scared I wouldn't get back to where I belonged, scared of being trapped in this strange time and place with a boy who was almost my double, and another boy who, though he didn't look like him, was another Brian. If I wasn't dreaming or insane, then I was on Ireland's west coast, in the middle of a famine that happened a hundred and twenty-seven years ago!

"I hope you'll stay," said Hannah.

She said it like she meant it, her voice solemn, her clear eyes looking into the middle of me, capturing my heart. That decided me: of course I wanted to stay.

There was nothing and no one to go back to anyway. No one would miss me.

. . . the riddle of time

God save all here," came a voice from the doorway. It was Fergus.

"Come in, Fergus, and welcome," said the father.

Fergus, fidgeting with his cloth cap, stepped inside. "There's Joan Hannay outside." He jerked his chin nervously. "And Mary O'Malley. They won't come in, but"—Fergus nodded toward me—"they wondered if the young feller would come out and lay a hand on the children. O'Malley has her youngest, Eileen, and Hannay brought little Timothy."

"Lay a hand?" said the father. "And work miracles? Are you out of your head?"

Fergus shuffled his feet. "I know, I know, Thaddy, but they asked me ..."

Hannah whispered to me, "Young Eileen is blind since the day she was born, and Timothy has the twisted foot and will never walk straight. The poor unfortunate mothers think you can cure them." She shrugged apologetically.

The father said to Fergus, "Young Tom Mullen is simply a lad who uses his fine English education and the common sense God gave him. Now go out there and tell them to go back to their homes and not be expecting miracles. Wait, I'll tell them myself." He struggled to get up.

"Stay where you are, Thaddy," said Ma. "I'll away out and talk to them. Leave it to me."

She went out with Fergus and I could hear her talking with the women.

"God help the poor souls," she said when she returned. "They're both of them up from Ballyhaunis these two years. Sickness and blight, and hunger and disease is all they ever saw. Miracles were never needed so much in this poor desperate country than they are right now." She turned to me. "After what you did for Tully, Tom Mullen, you need never fear the cold ditch, nor the wind and the rain, nor the lonely road with never the house or hut. There's a roof over your head here for as long as you need it."

"Indeed there is, and welcome," said the father, "though the Lord knows there is little to eat, no potatoes at all and only the bit of fish and dillisk."

"Thanks." I didn't know what dillisk was, nor did I care.

Right now, tired, light-headed, unable to think, I wanted to sleep. Later I would think. Later.

We bunked down on the floor that night, with our thin blankets and straw-stuffed pillows, Brendan and Hannah close to me by the fire, Tully, still suspicious and unfriendly, near the door, and the mother and father in the only bed.

Tully fell asleep. Hannah lay beside me, eagerly whispering a hundred questions, wanting to know about my parents, what it was like where I lived, on and on. I didn't mind, though my answers probably made very little sense because I was so tired. Brendan, on the other side of Hannah, was listening, also trying to stay awake with heavy eyes.

I didn't mention to Hannah that I was from over a hundred years in the future, because I didn't yet believe it myself. Her eyes sparkled in the glow from the fire. I told her about Brian, how we'd been together for more than three years, and how his bread wasn't baked all the way through, which, when I thought of it later, probably wasn't a very nice thing to say, considering the doughy condition of brother Brendan's head.

She looked puzzled.

Brendan seemed to be asleep, so I tried explaining it another way. "Brian's just a year older than me, but he can't understand things like other people. He's . . . slow in the head."

She whispered, "Ah, like poor Brendan, then! Touched by the faeries! God bless him. But it's a soft and loving heart our Brendan has, a finer gift than all the cleverness in the world."

Then she talked about herself, how much she enjoyed going

to school and meeting other kids—she called them childer—
from all over the island, how she wanted to win a scholarship
and go to a fine school in Dublin and be a fine lady like the
ones who sometimes visited Achill from Dublin and England.

"Mr. Gallagher, he's our teacher, says I've the quick head on
my shoulders and should go far if I work hard, so I do, I work
terrible hard—"

"Go to sleep, you two," said the mother.

Hannah smiled sleepily at me. "Thank you for bringing my
brother back to us, Tom Mullen," she whispered. "God bless
you and increase all you have. I will never forget the fine thing
you did for us this day." She closed her eyes and slept.

Now I couldn't sleep: the riddle of time and place was keeping me awake. I watched Hannah's small white face in the firelight.

Though there was no covering over the doorway, the one-
roomed cottage was warm from the glowing turf fire, but the
dirt floor was hard under me and I kept tossing and turning.
Because of the wind, there was hardly a whiff of the rotting
potato plants, so that was a plus. But I was still hungry and that
was a minus. Like the Monaghans, I had eaten a small piece of
fish, some seaweed—dillisk they called it—and a few boiled
winkles and limpets, which were small shellfish, the kind you
pick off rocks at the water's edge or out of tide pools.

I kept going over the events before and after the fall—if fall
it was—into the grave, trying to remember what it felt like, the
long drop into darkness, the scary guy—like a wicked goblin or
gnome—with his staff and lantern, the awful pains and the

lonely cliff, saving Tully, meeting the Monaghans. I worried about getting back, wondered if I was stuck forever here in the Dark Ages, stuck like a bluebottle fly in a pot of 1847 marmalade.

After a while I drowsily thought, It doesn't matter. Why worry? There's nothing I'll miss except the football. I thought about the other kids on the team and the two coaches, Greensleeves and Lanny, who keep us in line. I love football. It's the only thing I'm really any good at. And the kung fu maybe; I wasn't bad at that, though being small was a disadvantage, not having the reach with my arms and legs. They were all crazy about kung fu in Old Swan, mainly because of a new TV show about a Shaolin kung fu priest, and most of the boys, and some of the girls, walked and skipped about, chopping and kicking at the innocent air in front of their dirty faces.

I was dead tired but I couldn't sleep.

I'd only been away a day from 1974 but wasn't missing Liverpool. Did I mention how dreary it was in Old Swan? Except for maybe the North Pole, Old Swan was the bleakest place on the whole planet. There's always the same old biddies with their rain hats and shopping bags, chinwagging outside the Precky Road shops every day; the same beery old geezers shuffling out of the Cygnet pub and into Ladbrokes betting shop to throw away their few quid on the horses, and when the money was gone to sit on damp benches in Springfield Park mumbling to themselves all afternoon; the same boring kids plodding to the same boring school; the same old stuff day after day; who needed it? Bleak, like I said. And numbing. Excitement was making farting noises with your armpit in class while Mr. Baxter was talking, and then coolly, brazenly denying it was you. Otherwise it was all so flat and stale and empty, and so was the miserable fozzy, and so was Brian. He wasn't really my friend, even if we had been together for three years; he was more of a burden if you really want to know the truth, no matter what Hannah said about the finest gift being a soft heart, or whatever it was she said. I had no friends, or mates. You never made real mates in fozzies because it was like you were always competing with each other; besides, you never knew how long you would be together; so you kept your thoughts and feelings to yourself. I wouldn't miss anyone and no one would miss me and I certainly wouldn't miss Old Swan.

I stared into the glow of the turf fire, singing "Jingle Bells" to myself to help me fall asleep, which is something I've done, I don't know why, ever since I don't know when.

Here there was Hannah. And Brendan and Tully and the mother and father—a real family. Even if Tully didn't like me or trust me he was important to me because we looked so much alike. One thing was obvious: it was no accident that had landed me here; I belonged to this place in a way I couldn't explain, not like a fozzy, where you were just passing through.

Fozzies were a pain in the arse.

. . . Jingle all the way . . .

Hard floor keeping me awake . . .

The best fozzy I ever had was with the Feinbergs. Hang on a minute; not true. I wasn't with the Feinbergs. I was actually with the Bowells upstairs on the second floor, but you wouldn't want to know about them, a right pair of losers. The Feinbergs actually lived down on the ground floor and that was where I spent most of my time. They were very old. Mr. Feinberg smelled faintly of Lifebuoy soap and Mrs. Feinberg made chocolate cookies for me, special. I eventually told them about how I was discovered in Toys and how my mother ran off down Renshaw Street with her coat flapping.

"You remember this from when you were a little baby?" the missus had asked in astonishment.

"Not really, but that's the way I always see it in my mind."

Mr. Feinberg shook his head. "Poor woman."

I looked at him. "Poor woman? She ran out on me!"

"Maybe." He shrugged his shoulders. "But sometimes, when a ship is in distress, in a bad storm, say, they have to throw everything overboard."

"Why?"

"To lighten the load so she won't sink."

The missus nodded her head in agreement.

I thought about that for a while and then I asked, "Mr. Feinberg, are you saying my mother got rid of me because she was sinking?"

He thought, shrugged again. "Who can understand the human heart?" He looked at his missus and they smiled such sad smiles at one another that I thought if anyone understood the human heart then it had to be the Feinbergs.

Afterward I thought about it, and about Mr. Feinberg being such a nice old geezer, and I thought what he said about my mother sinking in distress was a crock of crap: she just wanted rid of me plain and simple.

. . . Oh, what fun it is to ride . . .

Tully got up to throw some turf on the fire and saw me awake. "They say the Devil never sleeps," he growled down at me. I could see only part of his face in the firelight; the rest was in deep shadow.

I said nothing.

. . . one-horse open sleigh . . .

He took a knife and a small piece of dark wood from his pocket and carved. I could see the piece of wood clearly enough but couldn't figure out what it was he was making. Probably another religious figure like the others along the walls.

"Why can't you get food from someplace else, like England maybe?"

He gave a dry laugh and crouched near the fire, keeping his distance from me.

"England!" he said scornfully. "Haven't the English tried their hardest to kill off the Irish these past eight hundred years! The gentry of Ireland are not Irish: they're English landlords, some living among us in castles and fine mansion houses, but many never setting a foot on Irish soil, controlling their stolen estates from across the Irish Sea. Aliens they are, every last one of them, renting their land to big farmers, who divide it and rent to small farmers, who chop the land into smaller and smaller parcels and rent to smaller farmers, who chop the land until it's no bigger than tiny potato patches to be rented to the poor Irish peasants at the bottom of the heap. But there are no potatoes and we have no rent to pay them."

"What happens if you can't pay the rent?"

His voice was harsh. "England is demanding higher taxes from its landlords. The more tenants and subtenants the landlord has on his land, the more he must pay in taxes. So the landlords are getting rid of their tenants. Our landlord's man is Mr. Begley. Begley sent eviction notices out months ago for everyone in the village to be gone by the end of September."

"The whole village?"

"Every living soul. But we're still here, for there's no place for us to go. We fear the military will drive us off. It has happened in other places, people run off their land by the peelers, the police, their homes tumbled to the ground."

"How old are you, Tully?"

Head bent, he continued carving. "Sixteen."

"And Brendan?"

"Seventeen."

I didn't ask about Hannah because I'd already guessed her to be about twelve. Instead, I asked, "Do you remember anything from when you were lying unconscious on the beach?"

He looked up from his knife work. "What is your meaning?"

"Did you have any dreams . . . or anything like that?"

He stood and took a step back toward his blanket on the floor. "If I had any dreams, then I wouldn't be telling the likes of you. Haven't you already conjured with my soul? Wouldn't I be the fool to let you muddle my mind!" He lay down again near the doorway and pulled his blanket up over his head like he was protecting himself from me.

My eyes were heavy. My question to Tully about his dreams had made him suspicious of me again, but I had merely been wondering, in a dazed and confused way, if his drowning self had called me here to save him, that we were connected to each other in some way. How else make sense of the fact we were so much alike, even down to the birthmarks on our bums?

As if he had been reading my mind, a harsh whisper came at me from Tully's blanket. "And I do not believe you saved my life. If there was any saving to be done, then it was the Almighty God Himself who did it."

Up yours! I thought.

"The ould women in the village bringing their troubles for you to solve!" He gave a scornful laugh. "Ha! They believe you're either a sorcerer or a saint. There'll be more yet, expecting you to rid them of their aches and pains, no doubt, fools that they are!"

"And cure their cats and dogs?"

"Like all the English, you must be blind. Did you not notice? There are no cats and dogs. There's not an animal left in the village; anything with the bit of meat on its bones is eaten long since."

"Whisht!" said the mother. "Sleep!"

. . . more like a bird

I finally slept, but woke tired and aching when Hannah got up soon after dawn and took care of the fire. Then the others got up.

My clothes were dry. Tully scooped water from a rain barrel and we stripped and washed from a battered basin outside the cottage. Tully, in a better mood, smiling and joking, mocked his sister in Irish as she washed, and she sloshed him a hard one on the nose with her wet washcloth. Bare-chested, Brendan danced about them, laughing like a five-year-old.

The morning was dry and bright. A cold west wind blew away most of the smell of rotting vegetation, but occasionally I got a whiff. Stinko! On the side of the hill a few stick figures of men and women dug weakly in the terraced potato rows, searching for potatoes, throwing blackened stalks and leaves onto a bonfire. A woman crouched over freshly dug potatoes, halving any firm ones with a knife, potatoes that hadn't yet melted into foul-smelling rot, searching for rare ones un-stained with the black blight.

"They'll not be finding much they can eat," said Ma. "It's better they'd be picking through the tide pools below on the strand."

There was no breakfast.

My back and hips ached from the hard floor; my thoughts were sluggish. Could I die in Ireland? I wondered vaguely. And if I died would I never have been born in the future? Never have existed in Liverpool? Was anyone missing me? Were the Two Peas, our "foster carers," asking Brian, "What have you done with Tom?"

Ma looked into the cottage next door and came out stony-faced, crossing herself. "The widow Mahone will live alone no longer," she said. "She is resting in the arms of the Holy Mother above."

Later, I watched as two men, their mouths covered, carried a coffin into the cottage. The coffin had been hammered to-gether out of scrap boards. The men were followed by two women. A short time later the coffin, draped with a piece of blanket, was carried out and taken to the burial ground on the side of the mountain where a small crowd had already gath-ered. There were two other coffins lying on the ground, also covered with blankets. Fergus seemed to be in charge, for he was ordering a team of gravediggers about in Irish.

"Who else?" Hannah asked Fergus.

Fergus nodded his head at the nearest coffin. "That's ould Dan O'Herlihy, the quiet, decent man. Didn't he up and die in the night from the famine fever. And yonder's the bit of skin and bones of a lonely wandering woman found early this morning on the road, God rest them both."

There were burials almost every morning, Hannah told me, to keep the famine disease away from the village.

The clouds were high and thin. The diggers straightened their backs; the graves were ready. The coffins were put down beside the open graves and several of the old biddies, seated on the flat tombstones, bent their foreheads to the stones and started wailing in high-pitched voices, one of them taking the lead, and then another, so that it sounded like two barrels of tortured cats, one group answering the other. All around the burial ground wrinkled old women swayed and murmured and cried with grief. More people came and still the wailing went on, other women joining in. Every so often the wailing died down and then it would start up again as a different old biddy took the lead against a background chorus of wails and chants. The blankets were removed from the coffins before they were lowered into the graves, and then the priest came and said a prayer while everyone kneeled, and still the keening went on in the background. All this time the men did nothing but bow their bared heads.

Brendan stood beside me, not taking much notice of the burials but eyeing the zipper on my jacket, his fingers twitching restlessly. I took off my jacket and gave it to him. He tried to put it on, but it was a dozen sizes too small for his broad back. He stood with it under his arm, happily playing with the zipper.

The men lowered the coffins, then shoveled dirt into the graves. When the priest had gone they passed jugs around amongst the men.

"It's poteen," warned Hannah, "homemade whiskey that'd rot your stomach."

I saw Tully taking a swig of poteen. He was with three other boys; two of them looked older, like grownups almost.

A man stood up on a tombstone and spoke for several minutes in Irish; he was talking about the widow Mahone's life, Hannah explained to me. Then another man got up and spoke in Irish about Dan O'Herlihy's life and the bad luck of the unfortunate lonely woman found in the road, and then he raised his bottle and took a drink before handing it down to be passed around. A man started singing a mournful song in Irish.

My heart leaped when I thought I saw the goblin man in the crowd, but when I looked again he was gone.

Tully went off with his friends after the burials. Hannah, subdued and quiet, took me over the hill and down to a wide stretch of sandy beach, noisy with the roar of a powerful surf. Brendan followed us, still playing with the zipper. I pulled off my runners and socks and walked with Hannah and Brendan in the waves. The wind whipped at Hannah's thin cotton dress and tossed her hair about her face. I got my jacket back. Brendan pouted. "Later," I told him. "You can play with it later." His homemade shirt looked thick and warm.

"You must be cold, Hannah."

"The wind is warm. Besides, I've cold blood, like a snake." She laughed.

"You're not a bit like a snake. More like a bird, I'd say."

"A bird is it? What kind of bird?"

"I dunno. A small bird, a wren maybe."

"The wren is a great one for talking and singing and getting into mischief."

"Then that's you."

"What about a thrush or a finch?"

She was having me on, but I wasn't sure. She pointed toward the cliffs. "Swallows are beautiful. See how they swoop and glide."

Brendan, copying Hannah, pointed up at the swallows and laughed.

"I'd love to be a swallow," said Hannah. "A wren is not so pretty but will do, I suppose. Am I as pretty as English girls, Tom, do you think?"

"Prettier."

Her face glowed. "D'ye mean that?"

"Of course."

She laughed. "Aren't boys all terrible liars, but it's happy I am that you're here, Tom Mullen." She ran singing into the waves and kicked water at me and I did the same to her and

Brendan joined in and we chased along the water's edge until we were out of breath and drenched by the spray from the drumming surf and our own foolishness.

We passed villagers fishing with handlines or searching the tide pools for crabs and shellfish.

She took me to a rocky place by the sea, to a small cave worn into the cliffside. This was their den, their secret place, she said. "It's where we played when we were little, isn't that right, Brendan? The three of us. D'you remember?"

"Secret place." Brendan laughed.

Inside the cave they kept heavy egg-shaped rocks worn smooth by the tide and used for bowling games on the strand, and there was fishing line wrapped round pieces of wood, and hooks for angling off the rocks. We sat awhile and watched Brendan playing with the rocks.

For the rest of the day we scrambled over rocks and sandhills and played and talked and laughed. Hannah taught me a marching song, in Irish, about a minstrel boy who went to war with his harp slung over his shoulder. By this time Brendan was looping his arm around my shoulder, calling me by name—Tom, come look at this or look at that. Tom, Tom, Tom, like we were old pals and had known each other for years. He reminded me several times that I'd promised to let him play with the zipper. We sat on the rocks and fished. Hannah caught a small rock cod. She was chuffed. She was so chuffed she threw her arms around me and kissed me on the ear.

7

. . . in fields not his own

Not so worried about getting home, and happy to be with the Monaghans, I slept better the second night.

The next morning there were two burials.

Afterward Tully spat twice on his hands and rubbed them together like he was preparing to do some heavy work. He grabbed a shovel and started digging sods of turf from the bog, which was what they called the wet, springy parts of the earth, while Brendan stacked them in the field to dry. I took the second shovel and helped. Tully said it wasn't a shovel, it was a slane, but how would you expect an Englishman to know that? Tully worked hard and fast. I couldn't keep up with him. The sweat poured off me. He said nothing to me except, "I can see you're not much used to hard work, English boy." I took no notice; if he wanted to act like a jerk, then let him.

After we washed, it looked like I was expected to go to school with Hannah. "What about Tully and Brendan?" I asked her.

"Tully will go down and mend the curragh," she said. "And Brendan is promised out to dig turf for old Mrs. McCallister, who can't do it for herself. Besides, those two big lumps are too old for school. Hurry, we'll be late!" I fell in beside her. She wore the usual black shawl around her shoulders, over the same faded blue cotton dress she'd worn yesterday, and moved quickly without shoes on her feet, skipping around the mud and puddles from last night's rain.

"Your brothers are hard workers," I told her, thinking of my blistered hands and how Tully had sneered at my efforts.

"Don't I know it well enough," said Hannah. "Tully has a good head on him but likes not the school. Brendan is a treasure. Too much of a treasure, Ma says, for anything he has he gives away, and works hard often in fields not his own. He is too kind-hearted altogether. And too soft to snap the neck of a screeching chicken if he was dying of the hunger himself." She smiled. "But I love him all the more for that. And Tully, too."

I wanted to say, "Then how come he acts like he's got a cucumber stuck up his arse?" But I couldn't say that, not to Hannah, so I said instead, "Tully isn't very friendly."

"He's only jealous of you. And he's terrible uneasy about

you looking so much like himself." She laughed. "He believes the shee-og sent you to steal his soul."

"Does everyone believe in the shee-og?"

"Not the men so much. But the older women, like Ma, and a few of the childer maybe, like Tully, who were told the stories of the Little People when they were small and took them too much to heart. They believe the faeries have the power of life and death over us, that they can spirit us across the sea to their home, Tir Na n'Og, under the deep ocean, where time stands still."

I thought of the goblin. "Can they make people slip back in time, do you think?"

Hannah laughed. "So they say. But it's all nonsense. Just stories, that's all." She looked at me. "Tully will soon come to his senses; take no notice; he has a good heart."

We walked in silence for a while. Then I asked, "How far is it to this school of yours?"

"Not far. It's in the Protestant Mission, but we Catholics go, too. Are you a Catholic, Tom Mullen?"

"Yeah, Catholic." Up to now, before meeting Hannah, I'd never really thought of myself as anything. I couldn't remember going to church with the Mullens, the couple who adopted me, the Mullens who gave me their name. Couldn't even remember the Mullens; I was too young. All I know is that Mr. Mullen was killed in a car crash, and his wife, who was also in the crash, ended up in the loony bin. The different fozzies I lived in for the first few years after that weren't any religion, so

I didn't have to learn every word of the catechism by heart the way the Catholic kids did—Who made you? God made me. Why did God make you? Don't ask me; if you ever find my mother, ask her.

Be a good boy, Tommy.

Then I went to a Catholic school for a while, Snally's— St. Aloysius's—and after that I had a break for a year at a Proddy—Protestant—school in Bootle before going to another Catholic, Snebby's—St. Sebastian's. Snozzy's was Catholic, and I liked sitting in the old church and looking up at the stained glass windows and just thinking about things because it was so peaceful and quiet in there away from the noise of the traffic, and on Sundays there was organ music and the sharp smell of incense and sometimes singing. The reason Brian and I were sent to Snozzy's was because the fosters, the Two Peas, were supposed to be Catholic, even though they didn't go either.

The wind was biting. I caught whiffs of the rotten potato plant stink. "Is it always this cold in September?" I asked Hannah.

She gave me a look. "Isn't it the end of October."

"But you did say it's eighteen forty-seven, didn't you?"

"I did."

We walked together in a comfortable silence under a cement sky, through the airy silence of the green, treeless landscape, and I thought of the suffocating stench and noise of Old Swan with its diesel buses and honking traffic and rubbish trucks and ambulance sirens. I'd never been in a place so quiet. We had left the village far behind and were on the moor under a huge bowl of sky, heading for a cluster of white buildings far away at the foot of the mountains. A bird rose up out of the heather with a sharp cry and flew off toward the cliffs.

I watched the way Hannah's fine brown hair swung about her head as she walked and the way a gust of wind would catch at it and hide her face until she brushed it away with hands like birds. She turned and caught me watching her.

"You're the strange one, Tom Mullen. You don't know where you are, or what month or year it is, and you look so much like Tully I can hardly tell the pair of you apart. Isn't it the remarkable thing?"

"How old are you, Hannah?"

"Twelve, the same as yourself."

That stung. "I'm thirteen and three-quarters, almost fourteen! A bit small for my age, that's all."

Hannah giggled mischievously. "I was only pulling your leg. Don't I know you're older. It's testing your temper I am, that's all."

"Well, I don't have a temper."

"Sure you do, indeed. Come on. Hurry." She sang as she skipped along, making me jog along beside her to keep up.

We came down off the moor into an unpaved street with a steepled church, St. Thomas's, the painted wood sign said. There were many well-built cottages with hedges of bright crimson wildflowers, and larger whitewashed buildings, all forming an L shape round a right-angled bend into an adjoining street. Hannah said, "This place is Dugort. Most of the buildings you see belong to the mission." She plucked a few ballet-dancer flowers from a hedge and braided them into her windblown hair. Then she stood in front of me, her blue-gray eyes serious. "How do I look?"

"You look very nice." She looked much better than very nice but I didn't know what else to say without sounding soppy.

"Have I them on right?"

"Yes." I wanted to touch them.

"I love fuchsias."

"And swallows."

"Yes." She looked down at her bare feet, then looked up guiltily. "Wasn't I only pulling your leg about the swallows." She smiled at me. "Ma says I'm the terrible tease." She fiddled with the flowers again as she looked down the street. A bunch of kids were playing in the street. One of them detached herself from the bunch and ran over to Hannah with an eager cry. Hannah said to me, "This is my best friend, Mary Coyne."

I gave her a nod. Like Hannah, she hadn't much flesh on her, and her plain pink dress was patched and worn. We walked together for a few steps and then I stopped before we reached the school. "You go ahead," I told Hannah.

She looked disappointed. "Will you not come in with us?"

"I'm like Brendan and Tully, too old for school."

"You won't go away? You'll still be here when I return home?"

I smiled at her and nodded.

"You promise?"

"I promise." She seemed fearful that I would disappear as

suddenly as I'd come, almost like she knew there was something weird about me.

I watched her thin, straight back as she walked with her friend toward the school. The wind caught at her hair, threatening to take the red flowers. Bare feet, slender body, graceful as a deer. She turned and looked back at me and waved, a solemn look on her small white face. I waved back, something I would never do in a million years if any of the Snozzy kids were watching: in Old Swan, girls existed to be ignored.

The wind blew one of the flowers out of her hair. She went into the school. I picked up the flower and walked back the way I'd come, but turning off the cliff path just before the village to stroll down to the cove where Tully had almost drowned.

The wind was stronger now and in my face. I could smell boiling tar. I stood on the cliffside and looked down. There were two kids in the cove: Tully and one of his friends, repairing the curragh, the boat made mainly of tarred canvas. Tully, seated on a rock, had the curragh drawn up beside him and was sewing a square of canvas over the torn hull; his friend was crouched over a small fire stirring a pot. The tide was rushing in and crashing on the rocks. Tully looked up, then bent his head, pretending not to see me.

I was still carrying the flower from Hannah's hair. I put it inside my matchbox, recently vacated by Michael Jackson, and climbed down to Tully and his friend. It looked like the friend had extracted tar from the same turf they used for their fires and was now painting it over the canvas on the mended boat. "Finish it off," Tully muttered to his friend, steadfastly ignoring me, getting up and turning his back as he looked out to sea.

"Hiya?" Like I was greeting someone in Old Swan.

The boy had a wild mop of black hair. He didn't stop working, but looked up and grinned at me.

"I'm Tom Mullen."

"Hello yourself, Tom Mullen. I'm Gerald Fitzgerald." He put out his hand for me to shake but, whether at the sight of his own tarred fingers or my likeness to Tully, hastily drew it back. "I've known you all my life, Tully," he shouted over his shoulder, "but you never did tell me you had the identical twin brother."

Tully glared at me like he was waiting for me to go. "I don't rightly know what he is, Gerry, but there's one thing I do know: he's no brother of mine!"

Eyeing me, but shouting to Tully, Gerry said, "So this is the young feller who saved you from your own folly."

Tully muttered angrily at his friend in Irish.

Gerry laughed. "Any fool who would take out a craft as light as a mussel shell in a storm deserves to be buried above in the churchyard." He grinned at me and winked. "Isn't that so, Tom Mullen?"

I shrugged.

"Is it a fool you're calling me, English boy?" said Tully, clenching his fists and stepping up to me.

I turned my back on him and started to walk away.

But Gerry had noticed my zipper. "What's that yoke you have on your coat, Tom Mullen?"

I demonstrated zipping and unzipping.

"Give me the try at it." Gerry laid his tarbrush aside and zipped slowly and carefully as if it might bite him, his dark curls under my nose. Then he slowly unzipped, feeling the metal teeth with the tips of his fingers, searching for the trick of it. He zipped and unzipped several times, each time with a little more confidence, then shook his head in wonderment. "It's a remarkable thing."

Tully pointed urgently to the cliff path. "Lookit!"

I looked up. Horses. Soldiers in red uniforms. Men driving carts.

"Dragoons!" said Tully angrily. "They're making for the village!"

"They've got carbines!" said Gerry.

Tully and Gerry leaped over the rocks and ran up the beach toward Slievemore. I followed.

By the time we got there the soldiers were already in the center of the village, still mounted. They were armed with guns and billy clubs. There were three carts, each loaded with six or seven men and stout lengths of timber. There was going to be trouble!

Everyone in the village had turned out, it looked like, to listen to a man seated on a horse. He wore a black suit and tall black hat and read in Irish from a paper in his hand. I couldn't understand a word of what he was saying but I watched the faces of the people in the crowd: they didn't like him and they didn't like what he was saying. They yelled his name, Begley. He had a pale face and tiny black eyes like pee-holes in the snow.

Tully's mother, father, and brother stood near the front of the crowd. Tully and Gerry joined them. When the man had finished reading, a great cry of anger went up from the villagers and they shook their fists at Begley and the soldiers and the men in the carts.

Begley barked an order. His men, a bunch of ragged low-life thugs, jumped down from their carts and began attacking the tiny stone cottages with the timbers, using them as battering rams to destroy the walls. I stood and watched, like my feet were nailed to the ground, listening to the loud violent thumps as the rams battered at the stone walls. Fights broke out as some of the villagers tried to stop them. The soldiers, still mounted on their horses, joined in, beating villagers' heads and shoulders with their billy clubs and rifle butts. Afraid of being beaten over the head or run over by the charging horses, I ran to join the Monaghans.

The yobbos continued battering the cottages. Stone walls collapsed in clouds of swirling dust. Some of the villagers turned their attention to the soldiers, pulling at their leather-booted legs, trying to unseat them from their horses. A fine dust from the broken cottages and from the dirt flung up from the street by the charging horses and the jostling crowd now filled the air like a fog. Shouts and screams. Some of the villagers were throwing the stones that had once been parts of walls. Tully and his father fought side by side with their bare fists. Brendan stood by helplessly, trembling, mouth gaping. A soldier, unseated from his horse, began beating Brendan with the butt of his musket or carbine or whatever it was. Brendan stood rigid with terror. I ran and snapped a fast kick at the soldier's goolies. He doubled over, fell, then clambered to his feet and pointed his rifle at Brendan. Before I could get at him for another kick I was swept away by the crowd. "Hit him, Brendan!" I yelled through the tangle of bodies. "Hit him!" Brendan lashed out wildly; his elbow caught the soldier under the jaw and he went down, this time to stay. I looked about me and saw Gerry pick up a stone and hurl it at the wreckers. The stone struck a man on the head and he fell.

I plunged into the crowd to help Tully and his father drag a soldier out of his saddle onto the ground. The soldier pulled out his pistol and fired. Tully's father fell to the ground. Tully screamed and threw himself on the soldier, hands groping for the gun. One of the other mounted soldiers, billy club raised, charged toward Tully. Coughing and choking from the dust, I hurled myself at his horse's head. The animal reared and swung away. Then a bomb exploded in the back of my skull and all I saw was black night and bright stars.

8

... catapulted back by a soldier's billy club

Twisting burning pains again, red-hot needles in my guts, but this time, out of the blackness and silence and the pain, there was music, like the old records the Feinbergs used to play, violins and flutes and a harp and a girl's light clear voice singing. Would have been lovely if not so much pain. Sounded like Hannah. Or an angel. I surfed on the wave of pain howling in agony as it swept me fast away before dumping me down hard on the ground, where I lay beached and broken, the sound of the girl's voice flooding over me.

Daylight but sky the color of lead, and Mullen in mud with coffins all around stacked sixteen high. The pit. The mass grave. I was back in Old Swan. I tried to rise from the mud but fell back and lay there, jaw clenched, while screaming molecules, torn apart in 1847, rushed to reassemble themselves.

When the pains went my first thought was of Hannah, her eyes anxious, suspecting something: "You won't go away? You'll still be here when I get home? You promise?"

Now I was back and I'd lost her. Hannah was gone.

My next thought was of the rumble in the village, Tully's father shot down, Tully attacking the killer, my rush to save Tully, only to be clobbered over the head. I explored my scalp, expecting to find blood, but there was none; head normal. Mired in mud, I tried to make sense of it all. But all I had was questions. Had the grave taken me to save Tully Monaghan? Was that why I was hurled back into the nineteenth century? Had the mission been accomplished and I wasn't needed anymore? Or had the mission failed when the soldier shot and killed both Tully and his father?

Now I would never know, for I'd been catapulted back to the Liverpool grave by a soldier's billy club.

Welcome home to Old Swan. Bleak City.

The music had stopped.

It was early morning, I could tell, because there were people coming out of Snozzy's morning mass and I could hear the old geezer who always stood at the church door with his collection box, chanting monotonously, "Peter's pence, Peter's pence, Peter's pence." The money was for St. Peter's in Rome. I used to think he was saying, "Peed his pants. Peed his pants." The church collecting pennies to buy clean trousers for poor kids who couldn't stop wetting themselves, which I thought was nice of them.

I rose reluctantly out of the mud, feeling like I had lost everything—Hannah, her family, freedom—everything. I'd never felt so rotten in all my life.

The music started again, a radio playing.

Camouflaged in black mud, I made for the end of the grave farthest away from where the work had been going on. There must have been hundreds of coffin stacks still waiting to be uncovered. I searched for a ladder, averting my eyes from stray bones and the contents of a few rotted coffins that had broken apart.

There were no ladders at this end, which meant I would have to climb up the coffins to get to the top. I gritted my teeth and started up one of the stacks, using my hands and feet the way a mountaineer climbs a rock face. But this was no clean, solid mountain: this was a grave filled with hundreds of decomposed bodies, human skeletons, and I was a worm crawling among them. Most of the rotted wood on the sides of the coffins broke under my weight and the pressure of my feet, forming rungs as I made my way up, but I avoided looking down and was soon at the top and out of the pit of death.

I crawled through the gap under the fence and was away from the grave before anyone, man or ghost, could stop me.

Back to the fozzy. Brian was there. He was chuffed. Tail wagging, he hovered jerkily around me, so excited he couldn't speak, his face shining with happiness under his helmet of black hair that spilled down to thick black eyebrows. Brian's is the same kind of big soft face as Brendan's except Brian's has got a curved beak, making him look like a giant finch, or a Norman invader time-slipped from the Battle of Hastings in 1066.

He must have wondered why I was so quiet—dejected more like, and stunned—but he couldn't know I was still back in 1847, coughing and choking in swirling dust, surrounded by a howling mob and soldiers on horseback.

I didn't want to be in Old Swan with Brian. I wanted to be in Ireland with the Monaghans.

I felt miserable as hell if you want to know the truth.

Did I mention that Brian is big? Like Brendan Monaghan except Brendan would be a couple of years older. Brian's strong as a gorilla. He's a year older than me, in a special class at school, but I probably mentioned that already.

And did I already mention the Two Peas? My brains are scrambled and no wonder. Anyway, they were given a special allowance as foster carers—that's what they're all called nowadays, not foster parents, but foster carers—of "difficult" or "problem" kids. Bent kids. Damaged kids. The Two Peas had no kids of their own. Percy and Paula Partridge were their proper names, a right pair of ball-headers let me tell you, but they were not the first fozzies I ever had with mashed cauliflower for brains, oh no. I could tell you stories, but you wouldn't want to know, they're too depressing.

Before the Two Peas I was with the Dodworths, which was

where I met Brian, him already there and hating it, I could see it on his face the day I walked in. The Dodworths were another couple with no kids of their own, in Aigburth, the other side of the city, but you wouldn't want to know about them either; they're just too dismal for words. Compared to the Dodworths the Two Peas were sane and normal. Brian and I ran away from the Dodworths but walked smack into a couple of coppers. They spotted us at the Norton Street depot trying to sneak onto a bus going to Oswestry, took us to the police station, and phoned Social Services, the SS—which was also the name of the top brass in the Nazi Party during World War II, the Schutzstaffel—I looked it up. The SS sent a pair of yobbos who twisted our ears and dragged us back to the Dodworths'. I told them about the nasty goings-on with the Dodworths and they said they'd put in a report. A longtime witness of SS rot and in-efficiency, I knew what that meant: nothing would be done for weeks. So we struggled along with the Dodworths and eventu-ally the SS got their act together and stuck us in with the Two Peas, which was fine, even if the Two Peas were a rough pair of sods. If you weren't home by ten at night they locked the door—we weren't allowed a key—and called the SS, who sent a goon over to grab you and lock you in a cell at the Juvenile De-tention Center—the Juvy—for the night, which was almost like home to me. And the next morning when they let you out Percy twisted your arm behind your back when nobody else was around until you said you were sorry and promised you wouldn't do it again. There were never any bruises, just permanent deformities—only kidding—but like I said, you wouldn't want to know about the Two Peas, so don't even ask.

We all lived together in the bottom-front of a big old wreck of a house that must have been a thousand years old, in Derby Lane, number 39. Paula's puppet husband, Percy, was big and ugly and strong, with Popeye arms and eyes like mouse turds. Brian was only a kid and he was strong, too, and I often wondered what would happen if Brian ever went bonkers, the way he does the odd time when he gets scared, and had a go at Percy, but it would never happen because Brian is terrified of violence. Percy spent most mornings at the gym sweating and grunting, working out with heavy weights. But Paula was the boss; she told Percy what to do and when to do it, while she either stayed in bed most of the day watching soaps or joined her mighty-mouth friends—all of them on the dole or welfare—in the back of Mersey Fish and Chips, gabbing and smoking and drinking coffee.

The Two Peas gave me a real bollicking, of course, wanted to know what I'd been drinking, what wet and muddy ditch I had spent the last two nights in, threatened to send me to the Juvy, said I was a sneak and a liar, a really rotten bad kid, not to be trusted, sure to end up a hardened criminal spending most of my life in jail—they knew all about my Juvy record, they said, but had taken me in out of the goodness of their hearts and also because they had built up a good reputation for dealing with hard cases—but it was no wonder my parents—if I ever had any—wanted shut of me, and on and on, you wouldn't want to hear the rest, it was just too depressing. Brian sat there listening to them going on at me, a big stupid grin on his face and his legs jerking and bouncing about like he had a live wire up his bum, but I could see just how chuffed he was.

Brian had kicked up a fuss, refusing to go to school without me. Once Brian digs his heels in, there's nobody can shift him, not Percy, not anybody, not even me sometimes.

"I'm gonna get rid of you two," Paula said to me. "You and Brian. You're more trouble than a nest of bloody rats."

She was still in her bathrobe at eleven in the morning, scabby-looking bare feet, curlers in her bird-nest hair, dragging on a ciggy and blowing blue smoke at me, cold, watery eyes glaring like she hated me, which she did, as if I cared, especially with the whole Monaghan business, the time slip and all, on my mind.

"Did you know we've been awake two nights trying to settle Brian down? Three o'clock in the morning and he starts yelling and screaming and carrying on, waking the whole house, bawling his eyes out because you wasn't home. Screaming about skeletons and coffins. 'The skeletons got Tom!' he kept shouting, over and over, whenever we tried to settle him. And of course, when I asked him what he was on about, he shut his gob, wouldn't say another word."

"Wouldn't say another word," Brian agreed proudly, nodding, rocking back and forth on his chair and grinning all over his big soft face. "Not another word."

We'd already missed the morning classes but I changed into my uniform—gray trousers, green sweater with the St. Oswald's crest—and remembered to take my matchbox out of the jacket pocket before I bundled up my muddy gear for the launderette.

Brian continued his excited babble all the way to school. "I didn't say nothing, Tom. Wouldn't say another word."

"You did good, Brian," I told him. "You're learning to keep your mouth shut."

You'd think I'd handed him a medal or something, he was so pleased. As we leaned on the school-yard fence, waiting for the afternoon bell, Willy Ardren spotted us and came over. Willy is a fat kid, school sweater too small to cover his stomach, belly button sticking out like a cork from a wine bottle, a real know-it-all.

Willy nodded toward the corrugated metal fence, ten feet high. "You heard the latest rumor? Now they're saying there's a mass grave in there, a bleedin' great pit, with hundreds and hundreds of coffins and skeletons."

I said nothing. Brian said, "Wha?"

Willy said, "That's why they've got a guard. Keep people from finding out."

We stared at the guard and the fence. The school bell rang. We started for the entrance.

"Tell you what," said Willy, "we could find out for ourselves whether it's a rumor or not. Meet here soon as it's dark, okay? There'll be a full moon."

"No thanks, Willy," I said.

"No thanks, Willy," echoed Brian.

Willy said to me, "You're scared."

"No I'm not."

"Not," echoed Brian.

"Yes you are!" Willy jeered.

"No I'm not," I said.

Willy sneered. "You're a yellow pisspot!"

I couldn't say anything back because we were the last ones in the door and Miss Hewitson, the headmistress, face like a swordfish, was standing impatiently on the top step, hands on hips, glaring down at us. "Hurry up, you lot!"

Brian smiled up at her. "You're a yellow pisspot!" he said happily.

9

. . . escape a certain death

I finally got rid of Brian in the lower hallway. "See you later, Bri," I said, watching him clump up the stairs to his classroom; then I turned and ran back out the door sharpish-like and headed for the Old Swan Library at Baden Road, pausing only to nick a chocolate bar at Hanbury's and an orange from Quik Serve. They could get along without me at Snozzy's a while longer.

The reading room was full of smelly old geezers reading the *Liverpool Echo* or snoring over a book. I took the big atlas off the shelf, found an unoccupied spot between the geezers, and turned to the map of Ireland.

Achill was a big island, part of County Mayo. Westport was

on the mainland to the southeast, about thirty miles. I located Dublin on the opposite coast, and then Liverpool across the Irish Sea. I shook my head in astonishment that I'd ended up so far from home, three hundred sodding miles away!

I put the atlas back and took down a book on Irish history. Altogether, a million people died of hunger and disease in the famine and another million and a half emigrated to escape a certain death, so the book said, and 1847 was one of the worst years because so many died of typhus and other diseases brought on by the famine. I thought about the Monaghans—though in fact I hadn't stopped thinking about them—wondering if they had survived the soldiers and the famine.

I sat there with the book in front of me on the table and I felt a dreadful sense of loss, like an echoing emptiness inside me.

Except for the snoring and sneezing and coughing and the rustle of newspapers, the library was quiet. There was no one to tell about what had happened to me and how empty I felt being back. Nobody. I could tell Brian but he wouldn't understand; he would think I was just telling him a story. Besides, I wasn't so sure anymore if it had been a time slip or something my brain had dreamed up while I was lying unconscious at the bottom of the grave. I had no proof. I'd brought nothing back with me but Michael Jackson's empty matchbox. But unlike normal dreams, which I never remember five minutes after waking, I could still remember every little detail of my trip, could remember freeing Michael Jackson into the weeds at the side of the dirt street, could remember the place, Achill, with its empty, treeless, green landscape and black sky and wind; the people, the faces of the mother and the father and Tully and Hannah and Brendan, every word they'd said, what they looked like—everything, including old Fergus and Tully's friend Gerry with the curly hair, and all those starving people and the smell of the rotted potato plants, and Hannah outside the whitewashed schoolhouse with the red fuchsias in her hair and the wind gusting and the promise I'd made.

Then I remembered Hannah's fuchsia. The matchbox *wasn't* empty. I slid it open. But all that remained of the bright crimson and purple flower were a few fibers and specks of dry dust and a scent like Mrs. Feinberg's face powder. The fuchsia had disintegrated. Still, I was certain, it couldn't have been a dream; whatever it was, it couldn't have been a dream.

I got back to school just as the bell rang and the kids were racing out down the steps.

Again, Brian almost threw himself on me, fizzing with excitement, like a big affectionate dog. We walked toward the Wharncliffe playground, Brian still twitching and bubbling, going out of our way only to nick a few pears and bananas on the way. When we got to Lahore News on Derby Lane, Brian had finished his pear and needed a chocolate fix. So he blundered into the busy store and nicked a Yorkie king-size, the bar that is "seriously chunky," while the Pakistani shopkeeper was busy. Brian was addicted to chocolate, especially Yorkie bars and Kit Kats. He didn't call them by their names, recognizing wrappers by their designs: he called them all chocky-bickies.

"How come you didn't come back to see if I was still alive?"

I asked him as he attacked his Yorkie. "I could've been lying down there two whole nights with broken legs; I might've died!"

"Wha?"

"The night we went under the fence, remember?"

Brian concentrated, scowling with the effort. "I remember, Tom. I remember all right. You fell in the hole. I remember."

Did I mention Brian's scowl? He scowled whenever he was trying hard to remember something. His thick bottom lip sausaged out and his black eyebrows flung themselves together like a pair of mating badgers.

"Then how come you didn't come back to look for me?"

"Look for you? I looked for you, Tom, I really did, honest, but I couldn't find you."

"You did?" I said, not sure whether to believe him. I couldn't see Brian going back to that scary place alone.

"I didn't just leave you, Tom! Didn't just leave you."

I looked at him, surprised. "You really came back?"

"I came back, Tom. I looked for you in the deep hole, honest I did, but I couldn't find you. I called and called and called but you didn't answer."

"You called? Didn't the guard hear you?"

Brian nodded ponderously. "Guard hear me, you bet. He helped me look for you, up and down, with his flashlight, up and down, but you didn't answer." He sounded hurt that I had doubted him. "Called and called," he said, eyebrows locked. "Looked all over for you, Tom."

I was impressed. It was brave of him. I wasn't sure if I would have been able to do the same.

"I was scared, Tom. Looked and looked and looked but couldn't find you anywhere. Thought you were hiding. Called to you to come out but you never did." He looked hurt again. "Why didn't you answer me, Tom?"

"I couldn't, but thanks, Brian."

All this time, Brian had been shuffling along, Yorkie long since vacuumed into his ever-hungry cake-hole, arms dangling gorilla-like as usual, grunting, his big head bobbing up and down as he pursued elusive thoughts.

After a while, he said, "Tom?"

"What?"

"You're not mad at me for not finding you, are you?"

"No, I'm not mad, Bri. Thanks for trying."

"Tom?"

"What?"

"What did Paula mean today? Get rid of us. What she mean, Tom?" He was almost in tears.

"Don't worry about it, Bri."

"She said," he whimpered.

I could see that this had probably been on Brian's mind all afternoon. "She's just saying that to scare us," I told him. "She's said stuff like that before. Take no notice of her."

Brian thought about what I had said. Then, "Take no notice," he repeated.

"That's it. Take no notice."

"They can't split us up, can they, Tom?" Brian frowned. "You won't let them split us up?"

"No, Brian," I said, "I won't let them split us up. Take no notice."

"Take no notice," repeated Brian. "I won't take no notice, you bet."

Percy was waiting for us when we got home, sprawling in front of the box with a beer in his big fist, feet up on a chair, starting in on us with his usual phony fozzy stuff. "Hello, boys," he said, sounding like our parish priest, Father Reynolds—Percy is a pretty good mimic, I've got to admit that—in his warm, caring voice. "Did you have a good day at school?"

"Sod off, Perce," I said.

Percy's mouse-turd eyes shrunk to tiny dots. "Watch your language, Shrimpo."

If there was one thing Percy hated, it was not getting respect. The funny thing was, he didn't have the faintest clue how to get it. He thought if he acted tough and bullied us we'd respect him. I think he honestly saw himself as a father to us two delinquents, wanted to set us on the straight and narrow, wanted us to look up to him.

I hated it when he called me Shrimpo.

Because Brian and Percy were so big, I was always reminded of how small I was—bad genes, maybe—but I was no shrimp. "Call me Shrimpo one more time," I said to Percy, "and I'll bust your face!"

He laughed at me.

I wasn't scared of Percy. There's one thing you don't do in a fozzy and that's let some ape push you around, no matter how big and tough he is. The bigger they come the harder they fall is my religion, and even if you get beat they leave you alone afterward so long as you did the best you could and didn't give in even when you were so shagged you couldn't lift your arms or feet. I'd never had to fight Percy, of course: he was an adult, after all; but if I did, I'd use what Lanny—did I already mention our football coaches, Lanny and Greensleeves?—had taught me about kung fu and get in some good kicks before he creamed me.

I hated being small. Which was why, whenever I got the chance, I ate as much as I could to grow bigger. I never got any bigger, though, and stayed skinny as a rat's tail no matter how many helpings of Paula's spaghetti I stuffed into my face every night. But I was pretty strong from playing football. Sometimes, when everyone was asleep, I slipped the latch and went out and practiced my kung fu and hung on the monkey ladder at the Wharncliffe playground for as long as I could till my arms felt like they were coming out of their sockets, and then hung upside down like a fruit bat, stretching my legs to make them longer, but so far none of it had worked because when I checked the last mark I'd scored with a bit of broken bottle on the telephone post outside the playground I was still almost the same height I was when I first got sent to the Two Peas more than two years ago.

"Stay out of the fridge and the cupboards!" Percy yelled after Brian, who had slipped into the kitchen. We weren't allowed to help ourselves. Paula would froth at the cake-hole if we did.

Brian poked his head round the door, whining, "But I'm hungry."

It took more than a pear, a banana, and a king-size Yorkie to satisfy Brian's appetite.

"Go play outside for a bit," Percy shouted.

I started for the door. Brian slipped back into the kitchen without Percy seeing him. Percy called, "Oh, Tom?"

I stopped. Percy stood and put his beer on the top of the telly. "Could we talk?" he said in his warm Father Reynolds voice, smiling, fooling me completely.

"What about?"

I sauntered back and Percy grabbed my arm and twisted it up behind my back before I knew what was happening. I yelled with the pain of it. I ought to have known. Being with the simple Monaghans had dulled my crap detector.

Percy whispered into my ear, so close I could smell his beery breath, "What about the last coupla nights, then? You don't fool me the way you fool Paula. Where did you get to, you little creep?"

"You're breaking my arm!" I yelled. The next thing I heard a crash and Percy screaming as he released me.

It was Brian: he'd smashed a chair over Percy's back. Percy never twisted your arm if there was anyone else around; he liked to do it without witnesses. But he hadn't realized Brian was still in the kitchen, probably thought he'd gone out the back door. Hurting and hopping mad, he went for Brian, who panicked, and rushed away around the room, wailing his head off with fear. I just stood looking at them, nursing my numb arm, while Brian blundered and stumbled, wrecking the place, table and chairs and cushions and lamps and all kinds of stuff flying and toppling. It was like a collision of two charging stags. "Leave him alone!" I yelled at Percy, but Percy was mad as hell and got Brian down on the floor and began punching him. Brian was strong but he didn't know how to protect himself, just lay there helpless, wailing and crying. I stooped to look at Percy's face; his mean little eyes were just about popping out like shiny glass marbles, he was so mad, and his comb-over— did I mention Percy's comb-over?—had flopped off to reveal his bald turnip head. "Hit him back, Brian!" I yelled. "Hit him back!"—flashing image of soldier pointing rifle at Brendan— Brian stared at me, eyes wild under his black helmet of hair, blubbering like a baby. Finally, to make Percy stop, I ran and gave him a fast hard kick, aiming for his chest but missing and connecting with his shoulder. The kung fu they do in the movies and on TV is always perfect, no misses, but real life is different. Anyway, Percy fell off Brian, howling with pain. I got ready to run before he murdered me but he just lay there, face white under his toppled comb-over.

Frightened, and worried about trouble to follow, Brian bawled for a long time after that. "Percy had it coming, Brian," I told him. "Don't worry about it."

Percy took a taxi to Broad Green Hospital and it turned out his collarbone was fractured and he would have to keep his arm in a sling for a month. Paula went ape.

But I was dead chuffed.

. . . smeared all over
with snot and tears

Red alert! The Two Peas were kicking Brian out. They would take care of me later, but right now they had to get rid of Brian. They weren't putting up with "uncontrollable, violent lunatics," who were "time bombs waiting to go off"—Paula's words —who destroyed furniture and put them in fear of permanent injury, not them, no way, they loved children, everyone knew that, they'd never fostered for the money, not ever, but they weren't about to risk their lives, not on your royal nelly, no sir, it just wasn't worth it, and on and on, you get the idea.

Brian got the message but it confused him: they were splitting us up. But best mates didn't get split up, did they? "They can't do that, can they, Tom?"

I wasn't thinking straight: the Monaghans were constantly on my mind and I wasn't over, and probably would never get over, a desolate sense of loss. And my feelings about Brian were mixed. I thought it was typical dirty work on the part of the Two Peas and I felt sorry for him having to start over at a new place, but he would be off my back; I wouldn't have to look out for him anymore. A big relief really. You've no idea how it weighs on you; it was hard enough taking care of yourself without a big softy to worry about as well. Brendan Monaghan was all right because he had parents and a brother and sister to look after him, but Brian only had me, and I already had enough trouble just trying to take care of myself.

Monaghans on my mind. Tully looking so much like me. Wanting to be back there.

I couldn't believe I'd never see Hannah again.

I kept thinking about their village being destroyed, about my broken promise, and wondering why I'd time-slipped more than a hundred years, trying to figure out what it had to do with all the coffins in Snozzy's school yard.

No one to ask; no one to tell.

Some days I felt like I was going bonkers, out of my mind, singing "Jingle Bells" over and over every night to fall asleep.

Brian would just have to get along without me and that was that.

Coach Lanny was cheesed off with me. "How come you missed football practice, Mullen?"

"Sorry, Coach. I won't miss any more."

"Yeah?"

"For sure."

Lanny's proper name was Lance Linacre. He was from Jamaica and was our junior coach, and he always looked sharp: shaved and scrubbed; neat in nylon tracksuit and polished football boots; shiny chrome whistle on a white lanyard around his neck; thin build, short kinky hair, green eyes, funny singsong accent. That was Lanny.

Lanny was another reason the kids were wild about kung fu. We all wanted to be like him. Poetry in motion—that was what our head coach, Jamie Greensleeves, said Lanny was. So we tried to copy him, even borrowing his "Keeya!" attack yell. Greensleeves took Lanny on as junior coach like, what, a year ago? So he could teach the team kung fu *and* football. Not only was kung fu good exercise, Lanny said, but it also taught focus and courage, and a whole bunch of other stuff. So in practice sessions Lanny always put us through a kung fu workout, even giving us homework—new moves and exercises for us to practice at home.

Coach Greensleeves gave me a wink and said to Lanny, "He won't miss again. I know Tom. If he missed a practice, then he had a very good reason. Tom would rather play football than eat, isn't that right, Tom?" He gave my shoulder a squeeze.

Coach Greensleeves has thick dark hair, grayed at the sides. Casually dressed in baggy football shorts, football jersey, boots with mud on them from the last time out, he was nowhere near as sharp a dresser as Lanny, no white lanyard and whistle, only a gold chain around his neck with something on it, gold cross probably, tucked inside his open-necked shirt. I liked him. He would tell you off sometimes, but only if you deserved it, and he was never mean. He loved the game. Lanny was tough and sometimes short-tempered; Greensleeves was mild and patient. They were like the tough cop/nice cop in TV crime shows. Everyone on the team wanted to be as tough and sharp as Lanny, but agreed that Greensleeves was more like a fond father to us all.

"That's right, Coach," I said to Greensleeves. "I just couldn't make it."

"Good enough for me," said Greensleeves.

"Well, don't just stand there," said Lanny. "Run out there and warm up."

So I ran.

"You won't let them split us up, will you, Tom?" Brian whined as we trudged down Derby Lane on our way to school. A cool, bright morning with a few high clouds. It was Friday, end of the week.

I ignored him. Except for a mug of sweet tea we'd had no breakfast.

"Tom. I'm hungry." Brian whining at me again.

"Hang in there, Brian," I said, my mind on you-know-what.

"But, Tom, I'm hungry."

He was starting to get himself in a tizz, so I said, "We'll nick a couple of fresh rolls from Sayers bakery, okay, Bri?" That was one good thing about Old Swan, lots of bakeries: on Precky Road alone there are two Sayers, a Greggs, and another one I forget the name of. The women who worked in Sayers were miserable, bad-tempered old bags, so that's where we nicked most of our stuff. The thought of food calmed Brian down.

But it didn't calm me down. That was typical, Brian nagging at me until I took care of him, a big helpless baby. It was like I had no life of my own. What was the point of being a loner if you couldn't be alone?

"Loaf of bread, me," said Brian, happy now at the prospect of filling his belly.

We were crossing Precky Road—Prescot is the proper name—at the busy five-way intersection with Derby Lane, Broad Green Road, and Snozzy Street, not waiting for the lights to change, daring the drivers to kill us, grinning like mad, and giving the finger to a bus driver who was trying his best to run over us.

We nicked an apple each from Kwik Save and chewed and chomped as we ambled along. Then Brian nicked fresh bread from Sayers while I kept the old witch busy, asking her questions about what kind of jam they put in their jam tarts, which she didn't answer anyway, yelling at me to mind my own business and if I knew what was good for me I'd get lost before I got a good clout over my earhole.

We got to the school yard with a few minutes to spare, our stomachs rumbling contentedly after half a loaf and an apple each.

"You won't let them split us up, will you, Tom?" said Brian for the ninety-ninth time, stomach full, no longer whining.

I wanted to scream.

"There's nothing I can do about it, Brian, but they'll keep you in Snozzy's, in the class you like. So there's no sweat."

"Wha?"

"It'll work out, Brian, don't worry."

"But we won't be in the same place, Tom. We're best mates, right? We been together a long time, haven't we, Tom, a long time?"

"Yes, we have, Brian, a long time."

"A long time, Tom," Brian said again, his hair like a Buckingham Palace guardsman's busby, blinding him. Percy tried to cut it one time and Brian wouldn't let him. "But you can't see where you're bloody going," Percy had nagged. "I can cut it myself," Brian said. He did cut it, taking the carving knife to it and lopping off the fringe just above his thick black eyebrows and slicing his thumb knuckle down to the bone at the same time. The hair on his head soon grew back again, but you can still see the white slash of scar on his thumb.

"It'll be okay, Brian," I said again.

I brought it on myself, the way Brian depended on me; it was my own fault for acting like his mother. Served me right. Be better if I ignored him, or told him to get out of my face, or made fun of him the way some of the other kids did sometimes, and maybe then he'd leave me alone. But he was right: we had been together a long time in the same fozzies—the Dodworths' and the Two Peas'—but did that mean I was like, what, his bodyguard? His keeper for life?

I was about nine, or ten more like, when I was sent to the Dodworths' and met Brian. He'd be eleven. I felt sorry for him,

I suppose. Poor soft-as-a-wet-sponge Brian; didn't know how to take care of himself. Terrified of the Dodworths he was, especially the old man, that silky, murmuring bastard. I could see right away what was up because he tried his tricks with me and I soon put a stop to it. Not Brian, though. I reported the Dodworths to the SS and they said they'd look into it, but they were too slow, as usual. So one afternoon after I found Brian sitting in the dark on the floor in his closet, all cried out, hair in his eyes, hiccups, thumb stuck in his cake-hole and his big dopey face smeared all over with snot and tears, I told him to pack his things because we were leaving.

"But where can we go, Tom?" he blubbered.

"Dunno. But I've got a bit of cash. We'll take a bus someplace."

"They'll find us and bring us back."

"Not if we're quick. Pack your stuff and let's go."

So we went. Like I already said, we didn't get very far, only the bus depot, before the police, wondering why we weren't in school, hauled us off to the lockup. But our attempted escape wasn't a wasted effort, because the last I heard the Dodworths were struck off the list. Bastards. Like I said, you wouldn't want to know about them. After that we were sent to the Two Peas; out of the frying pan and into the rinse cycle.

Now the Two Peas were throwing Brian out, and then me. "You won't let them take me, will you, Tom?"

That was like, what, the hundredth time? I didn't answer him. How could I? The chances of the SS doing something right and keeping us together were practically nil. My mind was already back in the past. Were the Monaghans in some parallel universe? Or had that all happened a hundred and twenty-seven years ago, and Tully and Hannah and Brendan were long dead and turned to dust like the flower in my matchbox?

I was like a zombie all day in school, pretending to work but thinking about Hannah, and about all the big shops in Old Swan—Sainsbury's, Iceland, Hanbury's, Kwik Save, their counters and shelves piled high with food while the Irish in 1847 were slowly starving to death.

. But 1847 was past and gone. Get your head straight, Mullen!

I promised myself I would skip school on Monday and search in the library for books that might explain what had happened to me. Why couldn't schools let you read whatever you wanted instead of everyone doing the same boring thing every day? I could have been reading about the Irish Famine, or out-of-time experiences, or could've been just sitting quietly, thinking about life. *What are you doing there, Mullen? I'm busy, sir. Busy doing what, Mullen? I'm sitting quietly, thinking about life, sir. Any conclusions so far, Mullen? No, sir, just that it sucks most of the time.*

Did I mention I was adopted by the Mullens? It was right after Toys. That was how I got my name, but I was with them only a few years. I was put up for adoption again but no one wanted a noisy four-year-old who dismantled the furniture and flooded bathrooms. It's all in my file at Social Services but you wouldn't want to read it, believe me, it's just too damn depressing.

Be a good boy, Tommy.

Well, I haven't been a good boy. I've been a little bastard if you want to know the truth.

At four o'clock repulsive education was over for the week, so I dragged myself out of Snozzy's and down the stairs into the buttery brightness of the September school yard, while everyone else about me rushed, yelling and screaming with joy.

Willy was waiting for me, but no sign yet of Brian. Willy jerked a thumb. "They're still taking 'em out." He meant the coffins. The guard was there as usual, standing with folded arms, watching the kids tearing out of school. "Here he comes," said Willy, meaning Brian. Brian had a big dopey grin on his face as he came down the steps. "Hiya, Tom?"

"Hiya, Brian?" I said. He was like an overgrown puppy. Greetings were important to Brian. He got hurt easily if you forgot to say "Hiya?" back.

"Hiya, Willy?" said Brian.

"Hiya, Brian?" said Willy.

"Let's go," I said. Willy tagged along.

We nicked some peaches and plums on the way to Wharncliffe. Brian attached himself to me as usual, offering me one of his peaches; I don't know why, but this irritated me.

We didn't stay in the playground long; Paula got mad if we played outside in our school uniforms.

Brian hung around me all evening, and even in bed he

wanted to talk. "You won't let them split us up, will you, Tom?" he whispered in the dark. Brian slept in one bed and I slept in the other—not real beds but green foam mattresses on the floor, with a four-drawer chest in between where I kept in the bottom drawer my magnifying glass for looking at leaves and insects and stuff, my *Science Facts* book, and my calculator. I got nightmares sometimes and wondered if Brian knew about them. If he did he never said anything. Did I mention I sometimes sang "Jingle Bells"—not out loud, of course, only in my head—to help me fall asleep? Especially after a nightmare. I thought about the scary goblin creature from my new nightmare, the shee-og or whatever he was, lantern and staff, glowing eyes.

"There isn't anything I can do, Brian, you know that. But there'll be no problem, you'll see." He was driving me bonkers.

"I couldn't stand it if they split us up, Tom."

It would be strange not having him around, following me, asking questions, copying the things I did. "You're lucky to be getting out of this dump," I told him. "The place they're sending you to will be heaps better, with lots of fries and chicken and hamburgers, and apple pie and ice cream, and king-size chocky-bickies and your own room with a big soft bed, wait and see." I hadn't the foggiest where they'd send him.

I couldn't sleep. When the house was quiet I slipped out of bed without disturbing Brian, grabbed my clothes, let myself out onto the deserted street, and dressed outside. As I hopped about pulling on my jeans, I could see through the window the couple in the basement with their new Pedigree pram, which they kept in the front room like a piece of furniture, and their new baby having its late-night feed in its mother's arms, and her husband bringing her a cup of something, tea probably. The young couple's names were George and Myrtle and their baby's name was Christopher. I stood in the street and watched the mother nursing her baby.

George and Myrtle put me in mind again of the Mullens. Whenever I thought of the Mullens it was all fuzzy. I remembered them leaving me, going away to Ireland, I don't know why, to visit relatives, or it might have been to a funeral of someone they knew who died. They wouldn't be long away, they said; they'd soon be back. They left me with old Mrs. Goss—I still remember her name—who lived upstairs, who let me choose boiled sweets, all different colors, from a fancy glass jar with a silver lid. I remember watching out the bay window from Mrs. Goss's second-floor flat every day, waiting for them to come home, but they never came. I took a sneak peek in my SS file a few years later and saw that they had crashed their car in a place called Glendalough, in County Wicklow. Peter Mullen died and his wife, Nancy, was taken to hospital. She ended up in the loony bin. I told all this to Mr. Feinberg and he made a telephone call and found she was still in the Rainhill loony. "Would you like to visit her?" he asked me. He came with me. We took flowers and chocolates. Scary place. People mumbling and groaning and wringing their hands. Nancy Mullen was an old biddy with gray hair, sitting in a wheelchair and staring out the window at the clouds. "Nancy, I've got a young visitor for you," said the nurse. "It's your boy, Tommy,

Tommy Mullen." I didn't know her and she didn't know me. She was right out of it, staring at nothing. Thanked us for the flowers and chocolates and wanted to know if we had seen Prissy, her cat, anywhere. Mr. Feinberg asked her questions about Peter, her husband, but she didn't seem to hear. She didn't have a cat, the nurse told us later.

I can't remember if there was a cat when I lived with them.

I didn't want to think anymore about the Mullens. It was too damn depressing if you want to know the truth.

I was still standing in the street looking at baby Christopher in his mother's arms. After a while I felt uncomfortable spying on them, so I turned away and set out for the Wharncliffe playground thinking about mothers, nursing babies, and closeness. Did that ever happen to me? Probably not.

The night air was cold; I zipped up my jacket and thought of Brendan Monaghan playing with the zipper. It felt good to get away from Brian and the Two Peas. Especially Brian; he was suffocating me. The bars of the monkey ladder were cold and damp. I hung on the bar for a while until my arms ached and I had to drop to the ground. Then I hung upside down by my legs for a minute, doing my fruit bat imitation, and the matchbox fell out of my jacket pocket. There was no need to keep it now that the flower had died. And Michael Jackson was gone. But I put it back in my pocket.

I performed a few kung fu exercises, starting slowly, stretching, chopping, kicking, finishing off with a few power leaps, aiming high kicks at the top of the monkey ladder.

The Wharncliffe streetlights painted the monkey ladder and

the edges of the empty playground the orange-yellow color of turnips.

Poor soft Brian. There, you see: most of the time Brian made me feel bad-tempered and nasty, but sometimes, whenever I felt sorry for him, I thought of him as "poor soft Brian." I looked forward to being on my own again; it would be great. I was glad he was going and that was the truth.

I leaped over the locked gate and was out of the playground and into the street.

I hadn't stopped thinking of the promise I'd made to Hannah, that I would be there waiting for her when she got home from school. I'd let her down.

And what *was* waiting for her when she got home? Her ma weeping over the bodies of her father and brother? Her home wrecked?

But what if I *could* see Hannah again!

The thought landed like a bomb.

I stopped abruptly in the empty street.

Supposing, just supposing, I said to myself, that I wanted to go back and keep that promise, how would I do it? Throw myself into the grave? Stand beside the grave and let it clutch me and drag me in like before?

I could try.

But then I remembered the pains and I stopped. I couldn't go through those pains again, no way.

But there was nothing for me here. Except a weekend of football. I wouldn't want to miss that. What would Coach Linacre say if I didn't turn up? Suspend me? Kick me out? No, he'd never turf me off the team, I was too valuable a player. Wasn't I?

I could see Snozzy's steeple in the distance. I started walking quickly, heading for the school yard, doubt and excitement fizzing up inside me. What if I *could* get back to Hannah!

I thought of the terrible pains and stopped.

Then the thought of Hannah propelled me forward again.

The school looked different at night. Scary. It was built in 1902—the date is carved in the stone right over the main entrance. Behind it, Snozzy's church steeple was silhouetted against the moony sky. Built in 1842, the church is much older than the school, and in daylight it shows its age: big sandstone blocks sooty black from over a century and a quarter of Old Swan's coal fires, tall pointed steeple pitted with shrapnel from old Hitler's bombs.

An owl hooted.

I was scared.

There was no sign of the guard. I ducked under the fence and made cautiously for the grave, my chest thumping. I could tell when I was at the edge because of the sweet musty smell and the blackness, thicker here like a black hole in the universe, sucking and eager to swallow me, pulling at me, pulling until I let go, and flew tumbling, already howling, downward into its dark yawning gob.

. . . on the skin of our feet

I dropped again to black weightlessness, into the glimmer of green light, while the madly grinning ghostly goblin looked me over, raising lantern, then staff, then came blackness and tumbling, and fiery pains just like before, a million needles in my heart and guts as all the tiny atoms and mollies in my body fought to realign themselves.

Unseamed.

Sick, howling and crying, I dry-heaved over the stones about me.

Morning light.

The pains went, leaving me clutched and smeared, head

thumping. Sliding through time is no joyride, let me tell you, no thrill. It is sodding painful if you really want to know the truth.

I looked about me. I was back in Slievemore, lying on the battlefield I had left, earhole sore and head aching. I rubbed my ear and my hand came away with flakes of dried blood.

But I was happy to be back. No, not happy, delighted, ecstatic, chuffed beyond belief. And so easy! Why had I assumed I could never get back, that I could never find again the thing I'd lost? Mullen the thick. Mullen the stupid.

I staggered to my feet. The soldiers and the yobbos had gone. Every cottage had been leveled. The street was strewn with stones that had once been walls, and thatch that had once been roofs. There wasn't a soul to be seen. It was like the end of the world. Nuclear wipeout. Even the early morning light seemed threatening. I wandered through the rubble looking for the Monaghans, trying to figure out which tumble of stones had been their cottage.

I asked an old biddy sitting in a broken cottage corner, "Where is everyone?"

She crossed herself and mumbled something Irish.

Then I saw a familiar figure. "Fergus!" I called.

He recognized me and made a trembling sign of the cross over his chest.

"Where is everyone?"

He shook his head. It was an effort for him to speak. "Most have taken to the road, or gone to the mission house. God have mercy on us. Wasn't Thaddy just buried this morning, let him rest in peace, so the missus is not yet gone; they're below in what's left of the house." He pointed.

The father dead, but the others still here. I clambered over the rubble and could see Hannah below at the wrecked cottage.

Hannah! I never thought I'd see her again.

And Brendan, but no Tully. I couldn't see the mother either. A small crowd of villagers stood about or sat on the broken walls, talking quietly. A few damaged Monaghan possessions had been rescued from the ruins and placed on the wall: broken crucifix, small wood sculptures, Sacred Heart picture, pots and pans, blankets and clothing. Then I saw Ma in a group of women; they all looked the same in their black shawls and skirts.

I can't describe how amazingly chuffed I felt seeing Hannah there.

When they saw me all talk stopped; the villagers fell back in awe, crossing themselves hastily.

Hannah turned and saw me. Her face was smudged from crying. "Tom!" she cried, throwing herself at me, almost knocking me off my feet.

Brendan came running behind her, laughing like a hyena. "Whooo, Tom! Whooo, whooo!" He jumped up onto what was left of the wall and capered about like an ape let loose from his cage.

Hannah clung to me. I could feel her heart beating against me. I said, "Sorry about your dad."

She stood back, eyes flashing. "Murderers! It's not enough

that we starve but they have to shoot us down, too!" she said bitterly, fighting back tears. "Where did you go? What happened?"

Brendan was still leaping and yelling.

She said, "Every living soul was out till dark looking for you. I thought you were dead." She noticed my ear. "Let me look at you." She steered me over to the broken cottage wall and made me sit while she went for a bowl of water.

Brendan hovered over me, worried, peering at my bloody head. He rested a hand on my shoulder. "Hello, Tom."

"Hello, Brendan."

"I worried about you, Tom."

"Thanks, Bri—Brendan. I worried about you, too."

"You did?" His big face crumpled in a smile and he stroked my back gently like I was the family cat.

The villagers watched me in awed silence. I glared at them and they crossed themselves again.

While Hannah washed the blood off my lughole, Ma came forward and put her hand on my cheek. "Welcome and God bless you, Tom Mullen. You're a sight for sore eyes. Weren't we worried you were killed."

"I'm sorry about Mr. Monaghan," I said.

She shook her head and her eyes grew teary. "May he rest in peace," she whispered. Brendan put his long arm about her. She patted his hand. "You're a good boy, Brendan."

Hannah was still working on my aching head. "Keep still," she ordered.

"What will you do?" I asked Ma.

"Ah! Tully is full of talk. He's wanting—"

"Mullen! Is it back you are?"

It was Tully, with Gerry, running down off the mountain at us, flushed and wild both of them. They had been drinking.

Gerry seemed pleased to see me. He gripped my hand and shoulder. "We thought we'd lost you, Tom Mullen, that you were killed. It was the fine brave thing you did, helping Brendan hammer the redcoat, and then jumping at the horse coming at Tully. Isn't that right, Tully?"

Tully didn't answer.

He still had the chip on his shoulder. Or maybe it was the booze working in him.

Gerry inspected my wound over Hannah's shoulders. He pulled a bottle from his hip pocket. "It's a drop of the good stuff you need. Here." He thrust the bottle at me.

"Will you leave him alone!" Hannah scolded. She laid a handful of leaves and flowers on the broken wall and started pounding them into pulp with a stone. Then she gathered up the sticky mess, slapped it on my wound, and began to bind it with a strip of bandage torn from an old dress.

Tully snatched the bottle from Gerry, took a long swig, and then shoved it at me aggressively.

I shook my head.

"Keep still!" said Hannah.

"Drink it like a man," Tully jeered.

I shook my head again.

"Be off, the pair of you!" Hannah barked at Tully and Gerry. She finished her doctoring. The bandage circled my head.

The villagers started moving away to their tumbled cottages. Tully held up his bottle. "May the good Lord see us safe and well in America!" He drained the bottle and hurled it into the ruins of the cottage.

I said to Hannah, "America?"

She shrugged. "There's nothing for us here, only hunger and disease." She nodded toward her mother, who was sitting on the low wall and staring off at the ocean. "Ma doesn't want to come, but we can't leave her here."

"How will you get to America?"

"A ship, of course. From Dublin, or Liverpool, whichever is best."

"And how will you get to Dublin?"

"How else but on the skin of our feet?" she said with a determination in her eyes and in the set of her jaw that I hadn't seen before.

. . . a fine life in america

The Monaghans left their village of Slievemore. Dublin was two hundred miles away. It was the afternoon. I went with them. Ma protested, not wanting to leave the village she'd lived in all her life, but Tully and Brendan took an arm each and helped her along while Hannah lured her with talk and promises of a fine life in America.

The sweet smell of turf smoke hung over the village of Dugort. There were no horses or carts anywhere, nor transportation of any kind, not even an old bike, though I didn't know if bikes were invented yet. The village was crowded with starving people. Across the street was Hannah's schoolhouse. Tents for the homeless had been set up beside and behind the mission house. We joined a lineup for soup and had to take it inside and listen to a sermon from a bad-tempered minister named Nangle who went on and on about popery and sin and other stuff I didn't understand. As we came out, a bunch of old biddies were standing in the street yelling at us, calling us Soupers. I was too tired to ask Hannah what the fuss was about.

We stayed the night crowded together in a tent, Hannah next to me on the hard ground. I woke up once and she was crying. She missed her father, she whispered, and was worried about her mother making it all the way to Dublin. "Perhaps we should stay here," she said, "and go no farther. America is the terrible long way."

I thought of Brian alone in our room, snoring his head off, and Paula and Percy in the room next to him, snoring their heads off, too, and old Harry O'Neill in the flat upstairs, and the young couple, George and Myrtle, with their new baby in the basement, and the old geezer who lived in the back on the ground floor, and the old biddy above him, all snoring their heads off so that a steady noise like a buzz saw stirred the morning stillness around 39 Derby Lane. But hungry and uncomfortable as I was, I was happy to be in Achill with Hannah—and with Brendan, and with Tully, too, even if he was acting like a jerk as usual.

I looked in my matchbox: no flower, only dust.

The next morning, before the sun was up, we set off walking. Hannah had recovered her determination. Hot, hungry, and knackered, we reached a large village called Achill Sound that had more beggars in the street than I'd ever seen, and more homeless people, and starving families with ragged, snotty-nosed kids. The main street ended at the sound, a narrow gap where the sea swirled and boiled as if in a cauldron. A crowd of people sat on the rocks across from the mainland less than a hundred yards away. Hannah told me they were waiting for the low tide so they could walk across the sound. Ma asked to be left there: she couldn't go on. We lay on the rocks and waited for the tide. Hannah untied the bandage on my head to let the air at the now-clean wound and then she and her mother fell asleep in each other's arms. Tully resumed his whittling, but, probably still feeling cruddy after yesterday's drinking, was soon snoring his head off.

I pulled off my runners and socks to let the air cool my hot feet. Brendan hunkered down beside me, looking worried. "Tom?"

Brian's whiny voice. I looked at him through half-closed eyes and saw Brian's big soft face and hulking shape.

"Tom?"

"Huh?"

"How far off is it, Tom?"

"What?"

"America."

I gave the question plenty of consideration. Then I said, "It's a long way, Bri—Brendan."

"More than a hundred miles, Tom?"

I thought about sailing ships. Were there any Atlantic steamships yet? I didn't think so. "Ships take a month, two months, Brendan. It's maybe *ten* hundred miles."

Brendan waved his hands helplessly, worried, unable to grasp so high a number.

"But England isn't far. You could stop there if you wanted."

That seemed to calm him. "Will you stay with us in England, Tom?"

I nodded. "I would like that, Brendan."

He smiled, just like Brian, like a happy little kid.

Hannah woke up. "What is Tully carving?" I asked her.

"A ring, like Ma's, from the same bog oak."

She saw my frown. "It's oak that's buried deep in the bog these hundreds of years," she explained, "and gone hard, like rock. Tully finds the odd bit of it when he digs the turf for the fire, and then his clever fingers must be forever carving it into something fine. Ma never had a wedding ring—Da couldn't afford it—so she asked Tully to make her one, which he did, and it's lovely. Tully has half the piece of bog oak left over—with the same grain in it—so I asked him to make me one just like Ma's. It's a Claddagh ring, which is meant to be passed on, usually from a mother to a daughter but often it's from a husband to a wife, or a father to a son, or, or a sweetheart to a sweetheart. Wasn't I just delighted when Tully said he would make me one."

People were starting to move. A rocky strand had finally appeared above the waterline and all the patient travelers, including several donkey carts and drivers, a herd of cows, and four big fat pigs, began crossing safely and more or less dry to the mainland on the other side.

"Leave me be," cried Ma when it came time to move. "I want to die here on my native soil. Leave me be!"

Brendan, almost in tears, hovered over his mother.

Tully and Hannah led her gently down onto the wet sand and over the barnacled rocks to the mainland and we joined a thin flow of people trickling slowly eastward. Almost all were barefoot; some limped along with the aid of sticks, some carried wicker baskets or pushed handcarts loaded with belongings, but most carried their bundles of clothing and blankets and snotty-nosed little kids tied to their backs. Most said they were making for Dublin and then England; others hoped to get on a ship at Westport bound for Cork and then England or Wales; all were fleeing from hunger and disease.

The countryside was flat and deserted and the weather was fine with a cold nip in the air. After an hour or so the road passed through a village of small sod huts built close together, many of them, as far as I could see, empty and abandoned. Some had dead or dying people inside, and were stinky like you wouldn't believe, worse than the pong in our Derby Lane bathroom after Percy's been sitting in there after a night of boozing and stuffing garlic pizza down his gob with his mates from the Cygnet. The smell in the village was from disease or dead bodies, or both; we didn't hang about to find out which. We hurried past a living skeleton of a man sitting outside one hut whose eyes had disappeared back into his skull and his shoulder bones were up around his ears, his skinny chicken neck having collapsed into his chest. He looked like something out of a horror flick. The village was a few miles from the sea, so famine conditions were worse. We hurried as fast as we could through the rest of the village and didn't slow down until it was a good way behind us.

My feet ached; I'd never walked so far in one go. And I was hungry. In the evening we came to a town called Newport. While the Monaghans drank and rested at the pump in the town square I nipped through the marketplace looking for food I could nick. There was nothing, only ground meal, the yellow color of puke and hard and sharp as gravel. I thought of Mersey Fish and Chips, Sainsbury's beef pies, heaps of apples and plums and bananas at Sainsbury's, just waiting to be nicked. But there was nothing in this small starving town to nick: I returned to the Monaghans empty-handed.

We spent the night in a ruined cottage with only half a roof, piled together like firewood for warmth.

We trudged to Westport the next day. It was a grind. We moved slowly. Ma Monaghan plodded without complaint, Brendan and Tully helping her as much as they could, me and Hannah carrying the bundles. Lots of people passed us. We went through places where everyone was starving. Ragged scarecrows twitched helplessly in ditches. Little kids sat on the roadside in a silent stupor, every rib starkly visible, no hair on their heads but thick downy hair on their faces that made them look like monkeys. You wouldn't want to know all the sights we saw, believe me, it'd make you weep.

We came on a tiny skeleton of a woman walking the road with a small boy. Ma spoke to her in Irish. The kid was sick, with paper-thin yellow skin shrunk and stretched over his skull, and eyes that stared at nothing. Looked to me like he was just about ready to kick the bucket, or pop his clogs, as Percy might say, except the kid didn't have any clogs. Brendan hoisted the kid up onto his shoulders and we moved on.

"God bless you," said the woman, hardly able to speak.

We got there in the late afternoon.

Westport was big and rich, and all hustle and bustle. There were the usual number of starving, homeless people, but there were also many shops and solid-looking houses, and fat, red-faced farmers, and carts rattling along the main road full of sheep and pigs and corn.

"There's no shortage of food here," I said to Tully and Hannah.

Tully was angry. He pointed to the stick figures lining the roads, some collapsed and unconscious. "You don't think these poor people are hungry?" Then he pointed toward the harbor. "Lookit! There's ships waiting to steal the food from Irish mouths! Every animal you see in those carts and every sheaf of corn are going to England!"

"But what about all those well-fed farmers?"

"They're the landlord's men. I'm ashamed to call them Irish," said Tully.

Hannah asked the way to the workhouse, and when I asked

what it was she told me it was a place that took in poor people. It would be a place to stay the night, she said.

The workhouse was a large brick building with steps up to a heavy front door. A bunch of miserable, starved, sick people sat on the steps.

Brendan was still carrying the sick boy. I helped the mother of the boy up the steps. Voices in the crowd said, "There's no room," and "They'll not let you in." A notice on the door printed in Irish and English said PUBLIC WORKHOUSE FULL. Tully knocked on the door, but there was no answer. He started to turn away, defeated, but I thumped a couple of heel kicks at the bottom of the door and kept striking until a big angry man came out and bellowed at me in Irish. He looked like Bluto in the Popeye films. Then he slammed the door in my face.

I kicked on the door again and this time when he opened the door his eyes were jumping from his head with anger.

"Couldn't you make room for just one more?" I asked him, pointing to the woman and her kid. "These people are sick."

He looked at them and I watched the anger leak out of him like air from a balloon. He said nothing for a while, and then: "I don't know where I'll put them, but come in, missus, and I'll see what I can do."

Tully and Brendan helped their mother back down the steps.

All I'd had to eat was yesterday's bowl of thin soup, not enough to keep a beetle alive. I knew now what it felt like to be hungry, really hungry. It sucked, if you want to know the truth.

The shops were a major disappointment: there was no food,

only the hard yellow corn again. We joined a long lineup outside a church for a bowl of soup that turned out to taste like toilet cleaner. I couldn't see how the Monaghans were ever going to make it all the way to Dublin on the skin of their feet without proper food.

13

. . . champion of mayo

The little man with the red hair and red face of a fox pointed to the prizefighter. "Do we have a challenger?" he yelled.

The prizefighter was a big, lumbering bear of a man, with thick shoulders and fists like wrecking balls. He strutted ponderously about the ring, stretching his arms and shaking his head. Sweat gleamed off him like he'd been slathered in oil. His name was Paddy O'Gorman and he was a professional boxer.

"Do we have a challenger?" called the foxy one again. "Come up, now! Is it fearful you are of a tired man?"

It wouldn't be long before the sun began its descent behind Westport Harbour. The crowd gathered in the field on the edge of town was hungry for more blood. The two previous challengers, their heads battered and bloody, lay recovering on the grass. Hannah, refusing to watch the fighting, had taken her mother to the church on the other side of town, joining crowds of other homeless travelers hoping to find a place for the night, but I'd stayed on with Tully and Brendan to watch the boxing.

Outside the ring of spectators were several horse-drawn carts containing animals: sheep, pigs, geese, a goat, a calf. There was also a booth set up to take bets.

One of the spectators, a rabbity-looking man with a clay pipe stuck in the corner of his mouth, seeing that we were strangers, explained the setup, aiming his lecture at Tully. "It's illegal, but the police are paid to turn a blind eye. Major Benson owns most of the land hereabouts. Lives in England. You see the man over there in the fine carriage?"

The carriage, parked near the betting booth, was shiny black, with a shiny black horse and shiny black-coated driver up front.

Tully nodded.

"That's Mr. Simmons, Major Benson's agent. Simmons likes his whiskey, they say, but that's his own business. More to the point, he likes a good fight. It's himself who puts up the prizes."

"What prizes?" asked Tully.

"Farm stock." He nodded toward the carts. "There's many the man will gladly take a beating to win a pig that'll feed his family for a month."

We looked at Paddy O'Gorman. There wasn't a mark on

him from the two fights. We looked at the poor wretches lying battered on the ground.

"He must be the great fighter," said Tully, impressed.

Rabbit-face held on to his pipe as he nodded toward the losers. "He is that, right enough. Strong as an ox. He's the un-defeated Champion of Mayo. But one of them two galoots—the big feller—won a sheep just for standing up to him for ten minutes. It was terrible punishment he took. Destroyed the man entirely. The other galoot didn't last five, so he got nothing but the bruises."

"Is that all?" said Tully. "Ten minutes?"

Rabbit-face laughed. "Aye! The longest ten minutes of your life while O'Gorman beats the tripe out of you!" He laughed again.

"Do I see a challenger?" yelled the foxy little timekeeper.

"That's Clancy, Mr. Simmons's bailiff. You don't want to get on the wrong side of that man, let me tell you."

"Come on, now," yelled Clancy. "The champ is tired, having already taken terrible punishment from two brave, stout Irishmen. And look at the size of this sow, will you!" He prodded a fat sow through the cart rails with his stick. "There's enough on this one'll last a family of four for six months!"

I looked at the faces in the crowd. Mostly men, there was a sprinkling of well-fed farmers, but the rest were a pretty sorry-looking lot, thin, starved, shagged; there wasn't one of them could punch a hole through a wet *Liverpool Echo*. The knot of men over at the betting booth were farmers or tradesmen who had never missed a meal in their lives by the looks of them.

Rabbit-face looked Brendan up and down. "You're the fine young blood. Why wouldn't you be the one to have a go at the champ?"

"Wha?" said Brendan, worried, hands moving.

Rabbit-face felt Brendan's biceps. "You've the strength of Hercules in that arm, so you have."

Brendan waved his arms. "Tully!"

"Leave him alone!" said Tully angrily, taking Brendan's other arm and walking him away from Rabbit-face. I followed.

"Are there no men among you?" shouted Clancy. "Lookit! I'll throw in a goose with the sow! How's that for you?"

Silence.

"I'll fight him," said Tully, raising his voice hardly at all.

I grabbed the sleeve of his shirt. "Tully, you can't. That bruiser'll murder you."

"I can take care of myself," he growled, shrugging me off and marching into the ring, which wasn't really a ring but a circular area of meadow.

I watched him go. He was strong, I knew that, having worked beside him, but he wasn't big. He would never survive ten minutes with a seasoned fighter, a grown man, twice his weight.

Clancy said, "Ah! Here's the brave one. There's heart in the youth of Ireland. A fine upstanding young man . . ."

"He'll not be upstanding for long!" someone shouted amid sympathetic laughter.

"He's too young," someone else shouted. "I'll not stand here and watch that thug beat a mere lad, so I won't!"

Tully took off his shirt so that he was bare to the waist, like the champion. But there the resemblance ended. Tully's chest, though well muscled, was slender; O'Gorman's was as big around as a barrel.

Clancy wasn't blind; he could see that it was a mismatch. He took off his cap and scratched his head, looking toward the carriage for directions from Simmons. "Tell you what. If this young hero can stay on his feet for three minutes, the goose is his. I can't be fairer than that."

"What about the sow?" someone shouted.

Clancy answered, "The sow is for ten minutes. But a goose for three is more than fair."

"A pair of geese," shouted the first man.

"Pair of geese," several voices joined in.

"Two goose it is," agreed Clancy reluctantly after a nod from the man in the carriage.

Immediately there was a crowd round the betting booth. I could see money and slips of paper changing hands.

Brendan whimpered, "Tom, what are they doing to Tully?"

"Don't worry," I said to Brendan, but I was worried.

"Come together," Clancy ordered the two fighters, "and begin when I step back."

It was like watching one of those old boxing movies where the fighters stand like statues with their bare fists raised high in the air before thumping away at each other, hardly moving their feet, until one of them falls unconscious to the ground.

Except Tully did very little thumping. It was all O'Gorman.

Clancy, peering at his big pocket watch, called out the time at the end of each minute.

With only three minutes, O'Gorman knew he had to finish Tully off fast, so he just bore in slowly like a tank and swiped him several ponderous but mighty blows to the arms, chest, and shoulders, knocking him off his feet—I counted—five times. But Tully was game. He should've quit but didn't. Instead, he struggled up each time, fists and arms protecting his head, standing toe-to-toe with the champ, hoping to beat the clock on sheer willpower alone.

When he got up after his sixth knockdown he was groggy, arms hanging uselessly by his sides. O'Gorman took careful aim and nailed him with a blow to the side of the head. Tully went down on his knees.

Brendan gave a loud cry of pain and struggled through the crowd toward his brother.

"Two minutes," Clancy called.

"Three minutes!" yelled someone in the crowd. "The boy stood up to him for the full three! Didn't I clock every second of it!"

Clancy said, "The watch stops for downtime; you know the rules."

"The full three!" yelled the crowd.

Brendan broke through the crowd and ran to Tully. Two men, Clancy's assistants, grabbed Brendan's arms and held him. "Keep back," yelled Clancy. "Let the dog see the rabbit." He and O'Gorman stood over Tully, waiting to see if he would get up.

Tully, trembling with the effort, began hoisting himself up but fell facedown on the grass instead. He tried again but couldn't make it and lay still.

Brendan threw off the men who were holding him, ran to Tully, and sank to his knees, yelling and crying fiercely.

I could see how the rules worked. There were no rounds, no count of ten. Instead, the fight dragged on to the time limit—the time a challenger stayed upright—or until he was unable or unwilling to rise.

I felt a white-hot anger flame up in me. Some champion! Punching a kid in the head. A few body blows would have been enough. He didn't need to show off his knockout punch on a sixteen-year-old! He was no champion. He was a bum. And that Simmons jerk wasn't any better, getting his jollies out of watching people get bloodied and beaten; what a sicko!

Clancy bellowed, "He's all right, folks. A bold young Irishman, true enough, and the great pity it is he only made the two minutes."

A roar of anger went up from the crowd. Mr. Simmons made a sign from his carriage.

"But to show you our heart's in the right place," said Clancy, his voice rising above the noise, "we'll let the brave young feller have the one goose, isn't that right, Paddy?"

The Champion of Mayo raised fists like hams and grinned at the crowd.

Brendan leaned over his brother's bare chest, trying to wake him, sobbing his eyes out.

It broke my heart.

And sent me plunging into the ring.

Thoughts coiled like a snake, I ran and struck, snapping a lightning low kick to O'Gorman's shin.

O'Gorman stood and looked stupidly down at his leg while I flew up like a bee and stung his gorilla schnozz with a hard chop, then flew back immediately out of reach.

His nose bled. He didn't know what to do. Clancy threw a towel at him and he clamped his nose, searching for a sight of me through the blood, too surprised to be angry.

The crowd hooted and yelled and laughed. "How will the Champion of Mayo handle the little brother, then?" somebody yelled.

O'Gorman started getting angry, shouting back at the crowd.

I slipped off my jacket and shirt, and stood away from him, near the edge of the crowd, waiting for him to come after me, wanting him to come, aching to hurt him. The anger I felt was so strong I could taste it.

Clancy, confused, looked to Mr. Simmons for instructions. Simmons shook his head. "Enough of that," Clancy shouted at me. "Away with you, little scamp, before the champion breaks your bones!"

"I'd like to see him try," I said.

That made O'Gorman angrier. A roar of merriment went up from the crowd. They were enjoying the spectacle of a kid facing up to the champ.

The laughter made me realize what I'd done. It cooled me off: temper and temperature zoomed to zero. My heart started beating wildly. I licked my lips, suddenly dry. I swallowed. I was scared. What a dumb thing to do! What had I been thinking of?

But I couldn't run away now.

Sure I could run away. What was stopping me? This ugly sucker would tear my head off.

Tully, sitting up now, looked stunned. Brendan, still bawling, was helping him on with his shirt.

Then I remembered Coach Lanny's words: "When the heart knows no danger, then no danger exists." And I thought of how O'Gorman had punched Tully: a full-grown man using all his strength to bash a mere kid! What a creep! My blood started to boil again. I tried to still my hammering heart and think of a strategy that would keep me upright, on my feet and out of the reach of those murderous fists for as long as it took to hurt the swine. I didn't care a damn about sheep and sows and geese, didn't care how many minutes I would last, and I didn't care if O'Gorman nailed me just as long as I got in a few good licks first. I wanted the crowd to ridicule him. I wanted to avenge Tully.

Boxing is fought close range, closed fists; kung fu long range, open hand or fist, plus legs and feet. Legs and feet could be deadly; I would have an advantage. But if he hit me only once it'd be game over.

I considered some of the strategies Lanny had taught us— praying mantis, flying crane, drunken monkey—as I glared into O'Gorman's mean little eyes. He was mad. He wanted to kill me. He threw away the bloody towel and came after me slowly, huge fists clenched, upright in his boxing stance, leading with the left leg, left fist.

He was going to send me into orbit. Like Apollo 11: Mullen to the moon.

Clancy tried to stop him, grabbing his arm. "That's enough, Paddy. Leave the lad alone."

O'Gorman shrugged him off angrily and kept coming at me.

I knew how he fought. Left foot leading, left jabs mostly. Strategy would have to be fair, clean, simple. Forget about the groin, forget about sweeps, trips, and flips. Concentrate instead on poking and evading, on lightning-quick hops forward under the elbows and big fists, attacking only the legs, then retreating from danger.

White crane: grace and self-control.

Praying mantis: speed and patience.

I circled to his right, forcing him to keep turning to find me. This strategy made it easier for me to defend myself.

Stay cool, I told myself. Yield and overcome. The supple willow suffers no harm from the violent storm. It was like Lanny was whispering in my lughole.

I circled casually, keeping him off balance.

The crowd laughed to see me so cool in the spotlight of the champion's anger.

Unaccustomed to turning and seeking, he was slow and confused; his opponents always stood squarely in front of him, fists and forearms in front of the head. So I got behind him and launched a flying crane to the small of his back. He staggered forward, then wheeled around, an expression of shock and disbelief on his face. I followed up with a hop attack—fast hop in, kick a knee, fast hop out.

O'Gorman was down on one knee, roaring with pain or anger, I couldn't tell which. The crowd went giddy with delight.

Howls of joy. "The more power to you, laddie!"

From the corner of my eye I saw a man cross himself. "God bless the work!" he bellowed at me from the betting booth.

I waited, horse stance, for O'Gorman to rise.

If only Lanny could see me now.

"Time's up!" yelled Clancy. "The boy has a goose."

No more than a minute had gone by.

"You're a cheat and a liar, Clancy!" someone yelled.

"Fight on!" yelled the crowd.

"The Irish soldier boy," someone sang.

O'Gorman, ignoring Clancy, stood, bunched his fists, and came after me, thirsting to thrash the life out of me.

I circled to his right, keeping out of reach, then switched to a left circle, confusing him. He was moving faster on his feet now, trying to nail me. I considered a high kick, but fancy stuff is not so easy, and it's risky, you leave yourself open; they might look good on TV but high kicks are hardly ever accurate against a fresh, moving target. Low kicks are faster and safer.

So that was what I did: I circled, hopped in fast under the fists, aimed a kick at the knee, hopped out fast, circled, stayed away. The snake strikes with great speed, Lanny always said. Legs can be felled like trees. Knees can be injured or broken.

The leopard leaps with speed and silence; the tiger, with tenacity and power. "Keeya!" I screamed each time I struck.

But mostly I circled, keeping out of his way.

I must have kicked his shins, knees, or thighs twenty-five or thirty times, retreating quickly after each assault before he could punch me.

The strange thing was that he didn't try to grab me, just kept those fists clenched, lashing out at me after I'd gone, tiring himself with the power of blows whistling through the air.

The crowd yelled with me, "Keeya! Keeya!"

Brendan waved his hands and jumped up and down. "Keeya, Tom!" he bellowed, the tears drying on his big soft face.

O'Gorman's nose was bleeding again. He staggered. His pins seemed weaker, but that could be a trick. I continued circling carefully to his right. Occasional feints with my feet had no effect: he just kept coming, lumbering after me. His arms were lower now, head unprotected, and I was tempted to try for a throat kick. Too soon. Too risky. I took advantage of another of his slow turns and flew in with a heel to his knee again. "Keeya!"

He was too strong for me to break his knee. But, groaning with the pain of it, he lashed out—too slow: I had already retreated.

His legs trembled. He stumbled and fell.

"Keeya!" shrieked the crowd.

He was on his hands and knees, starting to rise, so I

grasshoppered a reverse kick to his head, catching him on a cheekbone with my heel. "Keeya!"

"Keeya!" shrieked the crowd again.

I waited. I could see Tully. Bruised face, frowning. Then I saw my nightmare goblin, leaning on his staff, eyes glowing at me from the middle of the crowd, and my heart stumbled.

"Lookit!" howled the crowd.

I hadn't kept my eyes on O'Gorman. Stupo! He came at me, fists ready. I leaped and ran. Just in time. Mullen a pretzel.

A narrow escape.

Concentration. Discipline.

He was tiring now, I could tell by the way he was dragging himself. But I was pretty knackered, too; all that walking we'd done was taking its toll on my pins. I didn't know how much longer I could keep this up. Clancy had stopped calling out the time. I reckoned we'd been at it longer than ten minutes. Time might have run out, but O'Gorman wasn't about to let me escape.

He advanced slowly and patiently, noticing I was slowing down. But he was slower, too. I would have to try and end it. Time to risk a high kick.

I moved in like I was going to kick his knee from the front, but at the last second I swerved away to the side, then leaped back in and delivered a high kick to his throat. Bull's-eye! Just like on TV! He dropped to the ground, choking. The crowd roared. I heard Lanny's voice in my ear: "From the dragon we learn to ride the wind," so as O'Gorman shook his head and climbed slowly to his feet I rode the wind in a double cart-wheel, for show really—unlike in TV shows, fancy acrobatics hardly ever connect in real life—but got lucky and caught him on the schnozz again, this time with my foot, causing his nasal equipment to spring another bloody leak. While he was won-dering what to do I followed up with a flying crane, delivering a second fancy high kick to the chin. He stumbled and spun, then sat down, fists on the grass. I got in close and smashed the bridge of his nose with my elbow—Keeya!—hard as I could. "That's for Tully," I said. He screamed with pain and lay back on the grass, hands over his gob, and I knew it was all over.

"Keeya!" hooted Brendan.

"Keeya!" roared the crowd.

They went wild. "The sow is his!" somebody shouted.

"Wee champion! The good Lord increase all ye have!"

". . . pride of Ireland."

My heart almost jumped out of me I was that chuffed—Mullen triumphant—even more chuffed than the time I scored a hat trick against Sneddy's, top team in the league; I'll never forget that. Lanny would be proud of me.

Clancy was almost crying with emotion. "Take the sow," he said. "She's yours. Sure I never saw the likes of you in all my life!"

"I don't want the sow," I said.

"Then what is it you want?"

I pointed to the cart that had the sow in it: four iron wheels and a big sucker of a horse, chestnut-brown. "I want the horse and cart."

"You can't have it," said Clancy.

"I stood up to him longer than ten minutes."

"Maybe you did."

"And I beat him. I want the horse and cart."

"Winner chooses!" someone shouted.

"Give the boy the prize!"

"He deserves a pair of horses, never mind only one!"

People were shaking my hand, hammering me on the back, talking, babbling, asking questions, mostly in Irish.

"Come over here," said Clancy, leading me over to the carriage. "Mr. Simmons would like a word with you."

The crowd followed us over to the carriage.

Clancy introduced me.

"Ah, the young David!" Mr. Simmons said with a smile. He had a posh English accent, and blue eyes in a big red face. Middle-aged, graying beard and mustache. I don't know who told him my name was David, but I could tell from the way he spoke and raised his voice that he was playing to the crowd.

"The name's Tom," I said. "Tom Mullen."

He laughed. "Where did you learn to fight like that, Tom Mullen?"

I shrugged. What could I say—that it was all Lanny's doing?

"Acrobat perhaps? Circus work?" asked Mr. Simmons.

I said nothing.

"I enjoyed watching you fight," said Simmons.

It was the blood he enjoyed, I thought, men being beaten, but I said nothing.

"He wants Your Honor's horse and cart," said Clancy fearfully. "The big gelding."

He was keeping his voice low so the crowd couldn't hear, but those in front heard and started yelling. "The champion chooses the prize!"

"That's fair, Mr. Simmons!" someone yelled.

Mr. Simmons's smile revealed yellow teeth. "Then the new champion of County Mayo must have what he asks for, mustn't he, Mr. Clancy?"

Clancy's eyes widened in surprise.

The crowd cheered.

"Thanks," I said.

The crowd broke up. I started to follow them.

"Wait, young man. What age are you?"

"Thirteen and three-quarters."

He laughed again, like I'd told him a joke or something. Then he said in a low voice, "I can see a great future for you, Tom. Come in with me and I'll make you rich."

Again I said nothing.

Simmons said, "Mr. Clancy, be sure to give young Tom Mullen directions to the manor house so he may come and visit me tomorrow afternoon and talk business."

"Yes, sir." Clancy touched his cap.

I said, "Tomorrow I'll be on my way to Dublin."

Mr. Simmons smiled. "I think you will change your mind." The smile disappeared and he looked at me, cold-like. "If you know what's good for you." He tapped the roof with his stick and the carriage moved off.

. . . stars and fingers and eyes

Brendan was chuffed. He nearly squashed me to death.

Tully clapped me on the shoulder. "That was the most astonishing thing I ever saw, Mullen. You fought like Cuchulainn himself."

"Oh, yeah?" I wasn't sure what he was saying, whether he was accusing me of shee-og trickery, or if he was actually being friendly.

"Cuchulainn was a great Irish warrior," he explained.

"Well, thanks."

A compliment from Tully! What next?

"You did pretty okay yourself," I told him. "You won a goose."

Brendan kept yelling, "Keeya!" until Tully finally told him to shut up. But Brendan continued to bubble over with joy.

Clancy took me aside. "If you know what's good for you, young feller, then you will be here at noon tomorrow. Mr. Simmons is not a man to cross." He handed the slaughtered goose over to Tully. Then he had his men transfer the sow to one of the other carts and lead my horse and cart out to the street.

By now daylight had faded to dusk.

Tully admired the fine horse, shaking his head in disbelief. "It's a wonder. We should have no trouble getting to Dublin in this rig. Ma will bless every hair on your head, Tom Mullen, when she sees it."

He hung the goose on the cart, grabbed a strap near the horse's mouth, and tried to lead horse and cart away, but the animal wouldn't budge, looking him up and down contemptuously, the whites of his big wet eyes showing.

The street was crowded. Many of the men shouted congratulations at me and wanted to shake my hand. Tully got up into the cart and gripped the reins. Brendan and I got in behind him. The bottom of the cart was slippery with pig droppings. "Giddup!" yelled Tully at the horse. The horse didn't move a muscle. Tully noticed the whip lying in the cart and lashed a couple of good ones across the horse's behind. The horse dropped a load of steaming-hot manure into the street, then moved forward a foot or two. Tully lashed him again until finally the stubborn beast broke into a shuffle. That was as fast as he'd go, no matter how much Tully used the whip. But it was much faster and easier than walking. We stopped at the horse trough and pump in the town square, washed out as much of the pig dirt as we could, then made for the church.

Hannah and Ma were astonished.

Tully told them how we got the horse and cart. Brendan kept interrupting, babbling with excitement. Hannah raised herself up on her toes to examine her brother's swollen face while I waited for Hannah's approval; instead, she went the opposite way, thanking God for the horse and cart and the goose, then telling us both off for fighting: it was a sin, she said; we ought to know better; we were lucky we weren't killed.

The church was crowded, she said after she'd simmered down a bit. There was no room for them inside. People were being turned away.

It was almost dark, and a sharp wind was coming up from the harbor, cold as a witch's bum. I turned up the collar of my jacket. Lights shone from some of the houses, from lanterns. We stood in the street wondering where all the homeless people had disappeared to, the ones we'd seen in the streets earlier in the day.

"Have yiz no place for the night?" a woman asked Ma. The woman was very thin, and dirty and her eyes were glazed like she was more than a bit potty.

Too tired to speak, Ma shook her head.

"You're welcome to share our scalpeen so," said the woman.

The woman climbed into the cart and directed Tully to a field on the edge of town, and to her place, a hole dug several feet deep in the ground. Sticks and turf formed the roof. Inside, there was a man asleep. With Tully and Hannah, I took a closer look at him: stick-thin like a skeleton, he lay without a sound, the joints of his legs and arms swollen up like balloons and a bad smell off him worse than a boozer's puke. We got out of there fast.

We could see other burrows, or scalpeens, dotted about the moor, many of them with turf fires burning outside. Like a cuckoo looking for a nest to lay its eggs, we made the rounds, searching for an empty one. People sat by their fires or moved about in slow motion like they had iron balls and chains clamped to their bony legs. Many were sick, or dying, especially little kids, who were the ones hunger seemed to hit the hardest. One woman was wailing over the stiff body of a baby. I looked away.

It didn't take long. Hannah found a place. We climbed down inside. It would be a bit tight, but the five of us could sleep together out of the wind and the weather. It would do us for the night. There was straw on the floor, but it smelled a bit crappy, so we yarded it out.

Tully uncoupled the horse from the cart and tied him to a tree.

If only Brian could see me now, I thought. And if he could've seen me fight the Champion of Mayo. I felt light-headed with happiness. I'd never felt so happy. I was away from dreary Old Swan and the Two Peas. I was having adventures. I felt alive; I had power and freedom. And I had Hannah.

An old geezer came over from one of the other scalpeens and offered us half a sod of glowing turf, carried in his hands between two unlit pieces. He was thin and starved and weak, like everyone else. He spoke in Irish to Tully. Tully and Hannah thanked him as he placed the burning turf on the ground and tented the two unlit pieces over it.

"Thanks," I said.

"You're welcome surely," he said in English. He pointed. "There's more turf on the stack. Just help yourselves."

One thing about Ireland and its bogs: there was always plenty of fuel for a fire.

The mother cleaned the goose and cut off enough for a meal, in strips so it would cook quickly. Tully laid more turf on the fire and soon had a scorcher going. We sat around the fire, bellies empty, mouths watering, while the goose meat sizzled in its own grease, smelling as good as a newspaperful of Mersey's fish and chips.

Back home in Old Swan it didn't matter so much if you were sent to a rotten fozzy that didn't feed you right because you could always nick stuff from shops; no one ever needed go hungry. But here it was different: I didn't know how Tully and Hannah and Brendan kept going on nothing; and Ma, she never complained either.

After we had eaten, Tully, trying to make up for previous jerky nastiness by acting more friendly, showed me the ring he was carving. "It's called a Claddagh ring," he explained, handing it to me.

I peered at it in the light from the fire. On the front of the ring Tully had carved a heart with a pair of unclasped hands about it, topped by a crown.

"It's almost finished," he said. "There's just a bit more to do on the crown."

"And then it will be mine," said Hannah happily.

The dense, hard wood Tully was carving was dark, except for the heart, which had a smudge of buttery yellow grain running through it. I stroked the smooth grain with the edge of my thumb. "You've got clever hands, Tully." I handed it back to him.

Hannah grasped her mother's left hand, gently twisted her ring so the heart, hands, and crown faced front, and held it out to show me. "Ma's ring is identical, see? Cut from the same piece of bog oak."

It was finished, polished, but otherwise identical, for I could see the same buttery smudge of grain in the heart.

Hannah said, "The heart means love, the hands friendship, and the crown is for fidelity."

"What does Claddagh mean?" I asked.

"That's a village near Galway, where the ring was first made," said Ma.

The food and the fire had made us all sleepy.

Tully, stiff and weary from his beating, hobbled like an old man to the burrow entrance. I told him what Mr. Simmons had said. "We should leave early," I warned him, "before dawn. Before Clancy and his men come to take back their horse."

The burrow was warm but I slept fitfully, aware of the breathing sounds around me. After an hour of tossing and turning I crawled out and sat huddled over the fire, adding turf for more heat.

Cold. I looked up; the sky was clear and full of stars.

"That's a grand fire," Hannah whispered as she scrambled from the scalpeen and hunkered down beside me. "The goose was lovely."

She sat silently for several minutes, looking up. "What are the stars made of, I wonder?"

"Fire and gas, I think. Like our sun. The same. But most are bigger and hotter."

"Could people live on them, do you think?"

"No, not people. But most of them probably have planets whizzing around like ours, with people and trees and horses same as here."

"I didn't know. Imagine! The same as here!"

"Well, not really the same. Nothing's ever the exact same, no two snowflakes . . ." I took her hand and held it toward the light of the fire. ". . . no two fingers. Every fingertip pattern is different. Palms, feet, all different. No one else in the whole world has the same as you. Or me. Everyone is different."

"You and Tully would be the same, I'm certain. You look so alike."

"No. We're different." I looked into her eyes. "The patterns in your eyes are different, too, from any others in the whole world."

She looked at me in silence for a while, and then she said, "And you are very different, too. How is it you know so much? Working miracles on Tully's drowned body. And the fighting. Tully says nobody ever saw fighting like that, like a circus performance. The crowd went mad, he said, hungry though they were. Is it from a circus you are?"

I shook my head, though come to think of it, 1974 is a kind of circus sure enough.

"And now you're telling me about stars and fingers and eyes. You're a mystery, Tom Mullen."

I'd forgotten I was still holding her hand. I let it go. She pointed to the sky. "Look! A shooting star! Make a wish." She closed her eyes. After a while she said, "My wish is that Ma get well and strong, and we get to America safely and prosper there."

"That sounds to me like three wishes."

"What did you wish?"

"The same. For the Monaghans to be safe and well."

Hannah slid her hand back into mine. It was small and warm, like a pet mouse. "That was unselfish, Tom, not to wish for something for yourself."

I didn't know what to say, so I said nothing.

"I missed you so much when you left—after the house was tumbled. Tully missed you, too, though he would never admit it. You won't go away again, will you, Tom? I couldn't stand it if you did."

"Hannah, I don't want to leave you. But I might have to go. Suddenly. I won't know when."

My words alarmed her. She leaned her head against my arm and clung to me. "But if you *can* come back you will, promise?"

"I promise."

I tossed more turf on the fire and we sat together in easy silence for the longest time. I could hear the horse tearing contentedly at the grass.

Then Hannah murmured, "The horse will soon have us in Dublin. We've a lot to thank you for, Tom."

We sat holding hands and looking at the stars for a long time.

Then I got up from the fire. "I'll be back in a jiffy."

"Jiffy?" She laughed.

"I won't be long."

Nature was calling. But I should have waited for my eyes to accustom themselves to the darkness. I wandered off across the field, half-blind. The empty scalpeen I fell into was a deep one, so deep that it felt like I was falling forever.

. . . the creeping willies

Unzipped.

The gnomic one inspecting me by lantern light, mouth like a letterbox.

Black night, and pains chewing me up as zooming mollies home and settle. Red-hot needles in my eyeballs couldn't be worse.

You don't want to know about the pains again, they're too much, but when they eventually went I peered into the darkness. I could make out the dark silhouette of Snozzy's steeple against the night sky.

I was *not* glad to be back.

At the thought of Old Swan and the Two Peas a black depression fell on me like a heavy weight.

I closed my eyes tight, willing myself back again to Hannah, trying with all my might, pushing hard, ordering the grave to swallow me as it had done before. Snatch me! Wrench me back!

It didn't work.

A minute ago—a century ago—I had been holding Hannah's hand.

I climbed out of the grave as fast as I could in the darkness and stood at the edge and closed my eyes and jumped back in, avoiding the coffins and the skellies and landing with a jolt that drove the breath out of me.

No good. I was still in Old Swan.

Defeated, I climbed slowly out of the grave, which makes it sound like I was getting used to this and wasn't scared, but if you want to know the truth I wasn't getting used to it: all those bones and rotted coffins gave me the creeping willies.

Once out, I inspected myself as best I could in the darkness. No mud this time, just scalpeen dirt imported all the way from the west coast of Ireland. Who would believe it! I dragged my feet reluctantly down Snozzy Street and across Precky Road, hands and fingers tingling. It was about midnight, I guessed. One of the streetlights was out in Derby Lane, making it a bit spooky. The door was locked. I tapped at the window for what seemed like an hour but was probably only a minute before

Brian's pale face peered out at me; then he opened the door and I sneaked in.

"Tom!" He was almost crying he was so happy to see me.

"Hush!" I closed the bedroom door.

He hovered over me in a dither. By the time I'd got my things off he really was crying. "I thought you left me, Tom."

"It's okay, Bren—Brian. I'm back. What day is it?"

Instead of answering he grinned through his tears. "I knew you—I knew you—I knew you would. I knew you'd come back, Tom."

That was the thing that got me with Brian, his trust in me; his face was like a little kid's, the way it shone, especially if there were tears in his eyes like there were right now. I couldn't stand it, so I nipped out to the kitchen, grabbed half a loaf of bread and some fruit, and nipped back. I was hungry.

"Tell where you been, Tom." Wiping his snotty, tearstained face on his pajama sleeves.

"What day is it?" I asked him again.

He had to think hard. Then he said, "Sunday!" pleased with himself.

I had been away the whole weekend. I ate the banana but had to leave the apple because of pains in my stomach. Brian grabbed it off the chest between the two beds and sank his big horse teeth into it.

I flopped down onto my foam mattress near Brian's great apple-grinding bulk and closed my eyes. I was jaded. That's what Hannah said sometimes, in Achill, when her mother asked her to work: "Ma, I'm jaded," she'd say, slumping over like a rag doll and falling to the ground, pretending all the energy had drained out of her, and after a while her mother would say, "Ah, get up, Hannah, and stop your play-acting." And she'd help her to her feet and kiss her and send her off to do the job she'd asked for.

They would have the horse and cart. If they managed to get away before Clancy's men came they would get to Dublin all right, I was sure of it.

But that was more than a century ago. If they got to Dublin in the horse and cart, then it all happened many, many years ago, way back in 1847. Ancient history.

I needed sleep. My feet were killing me from my hard day of walking and kicking.

Champion of Mayo!

And after Dublin? America, of course. The Monaghans would sail safely to America.

Brian chomped his apple and chattered at me in the darkness like a bird.

Like a bird.

I'd wanted to be out of the flat before Percy got up, but he was already in front of the blaring telly, hunched over his sugar crisps, lapping it all up, cereal and telly both, goggling at *The Breakfast Show*, which is so phony with its loud loonies grinning and joking, like they're having the time of their lives. Percy was sucked in by all that rubbish.

Cereal and milk were on the table, so we helped ourselves. The milk was thin, made from powder. Without taking his eyes off the telly, Percy raised his voice above the level of the electronic noise pollution and said in his dumb croony voice, warm and phony, "So how did we get in last night, Tom?"

I didn't answer.

"Hungry, were we? Had ourselves a little feast, did we?"

Suddenly I hated it. I hated it all. I hated the phony blaring telly and I hated phony Percy and I hated this phony flat and I hated my phony life and I hated being torn away from the Monaghans. Even though they were dead and gone in the past, the Monaghans were more alive and real to me than these dead jerks in the present. Back there I was free. And I belonged—I was needed; I was important; I could do things; I was a somebody. The Champion of Mayo! Here I was nothing.

"I don't know how *you* got in, Perce," I said angrily, "but I came through the door. And the only feasts I ever saw in this dump are the secret pizza deliveries and tandoori take-aways you and Paula stuff down your fat cake-holes when we're in bed."

Brian looked scared. He didn't always twig on to what people were saying, but he could tell easily enough when they were angry.

Percy turned and threw such a look of hate back at me that I felt my heart freeze. I could see his hand holding the cereal bowl trembling, the one with the fancy new sling on it. "Your days here are numbered, smart arse! Brain goes this morning," he said, deliberately calling him Brain instead of Brian, "and you'll be next. How d'you like them apples, sport?"

It took a while for Brian to realize what Percy had said. "Where am I going, Perce?" he asked innocently.

"Wait and see," muttered Percy, regretting his outburst.

Brian turned to me. "Where am I going, Tom?"

"I don't know. But they want to move us. You first, then me. New fozzies, that's all."

Brian looked worried. "We'll be okay, though, won't we, Tom? They won't split us up, we'll stay together like always, won't we, Tom?"

There's a special word for when something's happening over again for the second time—daisy-view, or something like that. But I felt like it was all happening for the hundredth time. I said, "I don't know, Bri. We'll have to wait and see. But it ain't easy for the SS to find us a place together, you know that, especially when they lose our files and don't even know we're together in the first place." But I did know. I knew they were going to split us up; I could see it in Percy's leering gob. Probably told the SS we were a bad influence on each other. I didn't mind; I wanted to be rid of them all.

"So the wanderer has returned!" Dripping with hate, Paula standing in the doorway, smiling sarky-like at me, left palm cupping right elbow, splayed fingers of right hand waving cigarette. She was up early, and dressed in shirt and jeans, hair combed, cake-hole lipsticked. Unusual. Something fishy going on. She disappeared into the kitchen to make coffee; she couldn't operate, she always said, until she'd had her dose of nicotine and caffeine first thing, which for her was usually around noon.

"Time you were off," Percy said to me. "Not Brain, though. He's to stay."

I twigged but Brian was frightened and confused.

I said to Percy, "Didn't I mention? There's no school today. It's a holiday."

"No it isn't," said Percy. "Now get off with you."

I grabbed my jacket off the hook by the door. Brian followed me.

Percy said, "Stay, Brian." Like he was a dog.

Brian said, "Don't want to stay. Go to school with Tom."

I opened the door and just then a car drew up to the curb and a man and a woman got out. SS, the Nazis, you could spot them a mile off. The man was a goon. They'd come for Brian. The woman was young, and new at it, all smiles. "Good morning, Brian," she said, like she was there to take him on a holiday to Bermuda or the Canaries—it was probably the first time she'd ever laid eyes on him but she spotted him right away. "I'm Miss Nussbaum, your new family placement officer," she said brightly. "Are we ready, then? All packed, are we?"

"No," said Brian. "Not going."

I stood watching.

Paula came to the door with a holdall. She had packed Brian's few things while we were having breakfast, probably waited until we'd sat down and then darted into our room to empty his drawers and throw his stuff in the bag. Old cow. "Now, now, Brian," she said in the sugary voice she put on for the public. "Miss Nussbaum is here to help you. She wants to take you to a nice place not far from here. You'll like it, really you will."

"No," said Brian, and folded his arms across his big chest.

"You talk to him, Percy," said Paula.

"Now, look 'ere!" said Percy, pushing his ugly mug into Brian's stubborn face.

"Sod off, Perce," said Brian, unsure, scared, borrowing one of my swearwords.

"Talk to him, Tom," said Paula, pleading.

"Where are you taking him?" I asked the woman. I felt a bit sorry for her, being so young and new on the job. She was dressed in a suit, dark gray jacket and skirt, and you could see she'd got it specially for her job to make herself appear older, like a government worker. Nussbaum. Probably "nice bum" in German, which I guessed was what she had, underneath that stiff skirt. The goon was another story; he wore a blue suit but he was just an ugly goon.

"Mr. and Mrs. Smiley are taking Brian," Nicebum told me. "They're very good with . . . um . . . boys like Brian. He will like them, I'm sure, and they are so looking forward to meeting him." She smiled brightly.

"Where?" I asked her.

"Beg pardon?" Smile slipping.

"Where do the Smileys live?"

"Not far. Leinster Road."

I said to Brian, "Sounds okay, Bri. School mornings we could meet outside the Old Swan pub, bottom of Snozzy Street, right?"

Brian's eyebrows were doing battle. "Not going," he said to Nicebum. "Staying here with Tom."

"You got no choice," said Percy, sticking his schnozz in again. "You gotta go."

"I don't gotta go," said Brian.

The goon reached out and put a hand on Brian's arm. "Let's move it."

"No!" Brian wrenched his arm away, gave the goon a shove in the chest, and grabbed the jamb of the door.

The goon shot backwards and fell arse-over-tip into the street. Grunting with pain, he got up and tried to prise Brian away from the door, but Brian hung on like he was hanging off a precipice and if he let go he was a dead duck. Percy started pushing Brian from behind with his good arm. Paula and Nicebum stepped back out of the way, leaving Percy and the goon to wrestle Brian away from the doorjamb. They couldn't. Brian had a grip on the jamb and he wasn't letting go for anyone. His eyes were wild in his head. "Stop them, Tom!" he screamed. The doorjamb made splintering noises.

"Let him go," I yelled. "Let me talk to him."

Percy and the goon took their hands off him and stood back. I put my hand on Brian's arm. "You okay, Bri? Did they hurt you?"

Brian shook his head, his eyes starting out of his head in panic.

"Calm down, Bri. It's me, Tom. Everything's okay. Take it easy."

"Nobody will hurt you, Brian," said Nicebum. Nervous smile.

"Take it easy, Brian," said the goon. Like he was reading from a TelePrompTer.

"I'll be glad when he's gone," I heard Paula whisper to Percy.

Brian gradually relaxed his hold on the doorjamb, then let go and stood, arms hanging at his sides, blinking his eyes at me under his black busby, hanging over thick eyebrows. I tried a smile at him to let him see everything was okay. But everything wasn't okay; everything was definitely un-okay. I took his arm and led him to the car. "Get in the car, Bri. Everything'll be okay," I lied. "We'll still be mates, and we'll still be together, you'll see."

This calmed him. He climbed into the front seat of the car and the goon got into the driver seat and Nicebum wriggled into the back. Brian tried to wind the window down; Nicebum leaned over and helped him. "Still best mates?" Brian whined. "You promise, Tom?"

I saw Hannah's face. "Yes, Brian," I said, "I promise."

The car took off.

Paula gave me one of her snotty looks. "You're next," she said.

. . . see if my hands were clean

I missed the Monaghans.

I thought constantly, like an itch you've got to scratch, of my other, secret, life.

I was glad Brian had gone.

I was alone again.

The way I used to be, before the Dodworths.

I didn't miss him a bit.

On Thursday after school he was waiting for me outside and when he saw me coming down the steps his face lit up like I was the Easter bunny bringing him a whole box of Kit Kats.

"Hiya, Tom? I waited for you this morning, by the pub, just like you said."

"Hiya, Bri?"

I thought he wouldn't remember what I'd said about meeting.

"But you never came. I waited and waited. Late for school I was." His eyebrows knotted in anguish.

"I was late, too," I lied. "I'm sorry, Brian." I really was. I hated myself sometimes. "What's your new fozzy like?"

He shook his head. "You said you wouldn't let them split us up, Tom, you said."

"There was nothing I could do, Bri, honest."

His lower lip sausaged out. "They make me do sums."

"Who does?"

"And they make me read stuff."

"Your new fozzies? They make you—what?"

"I can't do sums, you know that, Tom, or read nothing, no matter how hard I try."

Willy Ardren and another kid named Tony Gill joined us.

"What's up?" asked Willy.

I said, "It's Brian's new fozzy. They're teaching him sums."

"And reading," said Brian miserably.

"Well, that's good, right?" said Willy, looking at me.

Tony Gill nodded. "Sounds like a good place."

"You guys go ahead," I said to them. "I'm supposed to go to Nazi Headquarters."

"What's up?" Willy again.

"Appointment. It's to do with me moving."

Brian started to come with me.

"I can do this on my own, thanks, Brian."

He looked hurt. "You don't want me?"

"No."

I left him standing, gawking miserably after me.

I didn't want to go to the SS office, so I went to the library instead to read about Ireland. There were signs everywhere saying SILENCE. The place was full of the usual stinking old geezers coughing and spitting and snoring. Some silence. The old biddy head librarian was on duty; she asked to see if my hands were clean.

. . . i get along without you very well

"Why didn't you keep your appointment yesterday?" Paula asked me on Friday, soon as I got in from school.

"I forgot."

"Liar."

I shrugged. It didn't matter. Nothing mattered. She nagged. I let her rant on; I didn't listen. She sat on the sofa, wearing a skirt and blouse for a change—it was Friday night and she was probably going out with her friend Melissa, another stupid cow—legs crossed and the usual cigarette waving about in front of her lipsticked gob.

Brian stood just inside the open street door, unsure of

whether to come in or not. Percy was out at the gym doing one-arm bench presses; his other arm being still in a sling.

"Well?" said Paula.

"Well what?" I said.

"Why didn't you go?"

"Go where?"

"To your appointment, stupid!"

"Didn't feel like."

"Well, you better feel like it on Monday or you're out on the street! Four-fifteen with your FPO. Be there!"

I shrugged. I'd probably go. Get it over with. Get away. Not have to look at Paula's ugly mug anymore.

She turned her attention to Brian. "And what are you doing here?"

Brian shuffled his feet and hung his head.

"Did you lose your way to your new home?"

No answer.

"Well, I don't want you coming here, get it? You don't live here no more. You live with the Smileys on Leinster, right?"

Brian nodded his head without raising it to look at her.

"That's where you go in future." She glared at me. "See to it he doesn't come round here no more!"

I said quietly, "You're a cow, Paula."

She started screaming blue murder at me. I got out of there. Brian lumbered along, asking me to keep the Paki lady in Lahore News busy while he nicked a chocky-bicky and then go to the playground with him, but I said no. "I got things to do,

Brian." I walked away without turning to say goodbye. I didn't want to see the look on his face.

I felt bad after.

I didn't care. Brian would just have to get along without me. I'd taught him a lot, the time we were together, survival skills. Like how to keep silent when people asked you questions you couldn't answer—how come you don't have a mother? Like how to nick stuff you needed without getting caught. Like not letting people boss you into doing things you didn't like, especially when they seemed extra-nice, stroking your hair or your leg and whispering things at you. Brian would have to manage on his own from now on: he didn't need me.

If I went to my FPO interview on Monday I could ask to be sent away to a different part of the city, some place where I needn't ever see Brian again. Get him out of my hair for good.

How come you got no mother?

Be a good boy, Tommy.

No proper name, just Tommy. There's nothing worse than not knowing who you are. It's like you're a nobody, like you belong nowhere.

I remembered when old Mrs. Feinberg popped her clogs. I was about eight, I think, or maybe nine. She was a really nice old lady. Cancer took her quick before she knew what hit her. The old man was broken up about it. Went round the flat like a ghost for the longest time, slippers slapping, didn't even do much reading, and he loved his books. He was a bald old geezer, with little tufts of gray wool round his ears, but he was gentle and mild in his ways. I asked him why he couldn't be my fozzy instead of the Bowells upstairs. He didn't have a separate room for me, the SS had told him. But I was with him till he died. I left the Bowells soon after that for a new fozzy, the Dodworths, which was where I met Brian.

I didn't mean to mention the Feinbergs, but they'd been on my mind quite a bit lately. I missed them if you really want to know the truth.

Did I mention that Mr. Feinberg used to sing as he worked around his little flat? One of his songs was "I Get Along Without You Very Well," from one of his old records, and I used to think he was singing about Mrs. Feinberg after she died. Anyway, I didn't think that was a very nice thing to be singing about her, so I asked him straight out. I said, "Do you *really* get along very well without Mrs. Feinberg? Don't you miss her?" I asked him that because I thought he missed her; I knew that *I* missed her; I missed her a lot.

He smiled at me and sat me down and explained that the song was about a man who missed someone he loved very much.

"But if he loves her, how come he says he gets along very well without her? I don't get it."

Mr. Feinberg explained that the man told himself he was getting along very well without her—except in spring, when everything was new again, or when rain dripped off leaves, or when someone laughed who sounded like her, stuff like that— I don't remember all the words of the song.

"I still don't get it," I told him.

"He misses her all the time," Mr. Feinberg said with a sad smile.

When I was alone I thought about the song and what Mr. Feinberg had said and finally I twigged. The song meant the opposite: he—or she—or whoever was singing the stupid song was saying that he *didn't* get along without her, that he was missing her like crazy! That made sense, because Mr. Feinberg really loved Mrs. Feinberg, anyone could tell that just by looking at them together.

I thought about my mother dumping me. I didn't miss her one bit! Not one little bit! I was getting along without her very well. If she didn't want me, then I was better off without her. I think she did me a big favor if you really want to know the truth.

Looking back, I can see now why he missed her.

Old Mrs. Feinberg, I mean.

She didn't ever say very much, neither of them did if it came to that, but he liked to sing around the place when he was doing stuff, or when he was in the shower, and the missus used to smile and wink at me and ask out loud if I could hear a cat being tortured somewhere in the neighborhood and what a shameful thing it was to hurt a poor dumb animal and whoever was responsible ought to be flogged, and I used to pretend along with her—I was only six or seven—saying it wasn't the screech of a tortured cat, Mrs. Feinberg, but the sound of the five o'clock siren going off at Jacob's biscuit factory. Then she would laugh and I'd laugh, too.

She was in Broad Green Hospital only a week before she snuffed it. He went to the hospital every day after walking me to school and just sat beside her bed, leaving at three to pick me up, then after supper we went together and sat by her bed watching her closed eyelids and unfamiliar collapsed face with the skull coming through. As we went down in the elevator at the end of visiting hours, Mr. Feinberg's eyes were wet. He never said anything, though, but always held my hand as we walked home together through the busy streets.

Like I said, she went quick, the missus did, and the apartment block wasn't ever the same after that. Mr. Feinberg was old and spoke with an accent. His family were killed by the Nazis. He escaped from Poland and came to England to join the Royal Air Force. He showed me a picture of himself with his mates standing beside their Wellington bomber, and pictures of when he and the missus were young, before they were married. They looked to me like totally different people.

When the old man snuffed it I felt like the world had stopped. I got home from school one day and found his door locked.

"Is Mr. Feinberg all right?" I asked Mrs. Sampson from next door.

"He's gone, Tommy," Mrs. Sampson said, face like a spaniel, sad eyes looking at me.

"What do you mean, gone?"

"It was a heart attack. I'm sorry, but it was quick and he didn't suffer."

"Where is he?"

"They took him to Broad Green but they couldn't do nothing."

I climbed the stairs to the Bowells' apartment and let myself into the empty place with my own key. I didn't cry. I was mad as hell.

After that I didn't bother going to school or to the SS. For about four or five months I lived on the street, sleeping in cars or in other kids' houses, and I did shoplifting and break-and-enters, all the usual stuff, and the police collared me and sent me to the Juvy for a few days or a week at a time and the SS would be there and they'd tell me to behave myself and I told them to go screw themselves and eventually I learned how not to get caught. But I got tired of living on the street and gave myself up and ended up at the Dodworths' with Brian.

One afternoon, soon after I got to the Dodworths', I was sitting alone in the silence of our poky little bedroom thinking about the Feinbergs and how much I missed them, and I don't know why, but after all the months of running and being mad as hell, I cried.

So now you know.

... circumstances beyond my control

I was fed up. And jaded.

I couldn't stop thinking about Hannah. And Tully. And Brendan and Ma.

Except for football there wasn't much to look forward to: a wet weekend, and then the SS interview on Monday with FPO Nicebum, when I would definitely tell her I needed a move away from Old Swan so I could dump Brian; and dump the Two Peas, and dump Snozzy's, and dump my whole miserable life.

I wasn't going to mention it, but they'd had me down in the headmaster's office on Thursday. Seems Paula phoned in and told them I'd gone missing. You'd think I was on the Ten Most

Wanted List or something. Miss Hewitson, swordfish face, asked me where I'd been, so I said I'd just nipped over to see some friends in Ireland, in a place called Achill on the west coast, and I was late getting back due to circumstances beyond my control. Is that right, now? she said. Well, they had all bent over backwards trying to make allowances for me but I was a smart alec who needed to learn a lesson. She put the word out to everyone, Father Reynolds, my teacher Mr. Baxter, the two women in the office, the school monitors, the caretakers, and St. Oswald himself and all the holy angels to keep an eye on me. I was a marked man.

Life was grim.

No way to treat the Champion of Mayo.

And it was raining; there was nothing worse than a miserable rainy weekend.

I worked it out that if I went back to the grave and got sucked in again, the same as I did last time, I wouldn't know where the Monaghans were. How would I find them? Win another horse and gallop away to Dublin so I could find their ship and watch them sail off to England? In other words, jumping into the grave again would be a daft, gormless thing to do because even if I tripped to 1847, (a) the Monaghans were no longer in Achill, probably no longer in Ireland, and (b) they'd be harder to find than a good fozzy.

On Saturday morning it was raining, like I said. We did a few stretching and kung fu exercises with Lanny (I wanted to tell him about the Champion of Mayo, but he'd think I'd gone bonkers), then afterward, in the first few minutes of the match

against Fazakerley—Fazzie's—I wasn't focused the way I usually am and their right fullback fouled me out of the game. A
big burly sucker who looked a lot like Brian, he came at me—I
usually play on the left wing, my left foot being as good as my
right—came at me like a runaway snow removal truck and
plowed into me. Go for the man, not the ball, was his religion.
I'd had lots of time to dribble round him, but I made the mistake of thinking this big bruiser was slow like Brian. End of
story. Ankle big as a football. I'd be limping for a week, Coach
Greensleeves said, and then I should rest it for at least a fur-
ther week before playing again. "You haven't been yourself
lately, Tom," he said smiling sympathetically. "The rest'll do
you good."

Lanny was cheesed off with me. "Serves you right. Missing
practices is not the way to avoid injuries, Mullen."

Up yours, I thought, but didn't say it, not wanting to be
thrown off the team.

After the game, which we lost three–nil, Greensleeves gave
me a ride home through the rain in his truck with Greensleeves Garden Centre painted on the side in fancy green
letters—it's his own business, trees, plants, gardening stuff, in
Thomas Lane. He wasn't really all that old either, middle-aged
more like, a quiet bloke, dark hair, blue eyes, slow smile, open-
necked shirt to show off his hairy chest, gold chain bouncing
on the curly hairs. Kept himself fit. Good with a football.
Which was all I knew about him.

He wanted to take me to Broad Green for an X ray, but I said
no, that it'd be okay once the swelling went down. "Needs

plenty of rest," he said. "Ice it every twenty minutes." He dropped me off at the Two Peas'. "Let me help you in, Tom," he said.

"No. I'll be fine."

"Take care of that ankle, Tom," he said, before he drove off. "Get it checked. We can't afford to lose our number two striker. I'll call later to see how you are."

Greensleeves calling me number two striker (an ace of a kid named Danny Brierley was our number one) made me feel a lot better. I limped in to find Percy watching the telly. Paula was out. Then the strangest thing: he saw me limping and took a look at my ankle. I couldn't get over it. Suddenly saw himself as some kind of sports injury specialist. Felt the swelling with his hand, the one at the end of his good arm, very tender-like, and said, "Ice is what this needs. Hang on." Then he went out in the pouring rain and brought back a king-size bag of frozen peas, wrapped it in a towel, bunged it on the swelling, wrapped a second towel round the whole works, and had me lie back on the sofa while he made me a cup of tea with extra sugar in it for the shock. Then he phoned one of his pals who came in his truck, and, no matter how much I protested, took me to Emergency and waited while I was X-rayed and afterward he and his mate took me back.

Percy! Who would have guessed? The broken collarbone must have gone to his head. Anyway, I let him spoil me; it'd never happen again.

Sunday was a wipeout, more rain and me sitting in with my sore ankle propped up on a cushion instead of kicking a ball around with Brian and a bunch of other kids over in Springfield Park the way we usually did on a Sunday morning. Percy's mother came to dinner at one o'clock and we all had to listen to her babbling on about the operation on her colon that she had to go into Broad Green for next week and how much she was dreading it and how a friend of hers, Mrs. Blurge in Albany Road, had it done and how painful and uncomfortable it was. After dinner Mrs. Partridge went home, and the Two Peas spent the rest of the afternoon arguing about the way Percy's mother only ever wanted to talk about herself, and who wanted to hear all about her insides anyway? It was disgusting. And about how well her older son, Wilfred, was doing with his butcher shop, which was a way of putting Percy down—Wilfred didn't waste his time in the gym every day—and about how Paula had ruined a perfectly good leg of lamb by having the oven up too high and drying it out until it tasted like plastic. I limped to my room, which I had all to myself now, looked up colon in my *Science Facts*, and saw pictures of Mrs. Partridge's digestive system, which, believe me, you wouldn't want to know about.

Brian came round about half-three to see if I wanted to go out. Paula answered the door and told him I'd busted my ankle and couldn't walk, which wasn't quite true, it wasn't broken, only sprained. She closed the door on him without asking him in. I didn't care.

There was no way I was going to hang about the house all day Monday, so I started for school. Old Harry O'Neill in the flat upstairs was leaning out his window. He saw me limping and yelled, "Whassamatter with yer leg?"

"Sprained ankle," I yelled back.

"Wait a minute, boy!" His head disappeared and when it came back a cane came with it. "Catch!" he said, throwing it down to me. He walked with a cane all the time, had a selection of several different ones. "Thanks very much," I said.

I walked to school with my cane, looking like Harold Wilson, the Prime Minister.

After school, Nicebum asked about my foot, then found my file in the cabinet and sat behind her desk looking through it.

I looked around. Files everywhere, in stacks on the cabinets, in piles on the floor. The place was a mess even though Nicebum had obviously started to try and clean it up. There was a new cabinet in the corner that wasn't there when my last FPO had the office.

Nicebum was frowning over my file.

I knew what was in my file, most of it anyway. "Subject's History," that's what most of it was called. I was the subject. Because it was December 16—close to Christmas—when I was found, and because I was reckoned to be about a year old at the time, the SS put that down as my birthday. Which meant I would be fourteen in about three months from now.

Then there was the part I called my rap sheet, which listed all my crimes against humanity—the ones they'd caught me for—and how long I spent in the Juvy, all the dates, the reports of police and court officers and social service workers and family placement officers all clipped together in hysterical order.

Nicebum asked me a whole bunch of questions, like where I would like to live.

"New York."

She smiled. "Why New York?"

I liked her smile. Blue-gray eyes, reminded me of Hannah. "Big. Busy. Get lost. Nobody bother you."

"Where else would you like to live that's closer?"

"Robin Hood's Bay."

"Be serious," she said, still smiling. She was more relaxed when there were no SS goons around. Her jacket hung on the back of her chair and she wore a nice crispy white shirt.

"I am serious."

"But that's in Yorkshire."

"I know," I said. "But I've seen pictures and it looks a nice place."

She then got boring, explaining how they liked to keep kids in the same district, at the same school, blah blah blah, I'd heard it all before, so I let her yak on while I turned my thoughts to more interesting things like the shape of her chest (protuberant, a neat word from *Science Facts*), shape of her mouth (smiley), and the color of her eyes, and the way one eyebrow sometimes went up, stuff like that. She saw me gawking at her and she blushed and I felt like a right stupid wally.

When she paused for a breath I told her it would be in my best interest—using one of her own phrases—for me to move to a different district because too many of the no-good yahoos and yobbos I knew from the Juvy lived in Old Swan and they were a bad influence on me and that was why I'd gone missing, though I couldn't possibly tell her what they made me do, and on and on, you get the idea, all of it a pack of lies from beginning to end, but I was very convincing and she believed me. I was cunning all right.

She couldn't promise anything, for any transfer she made had to be approved by her boss, she said, but agreed in the end to try to find me a place in a different district even though it would mean moving to a new school and the SS having to fork out for a new school uniform, which I knew to be a bunch of rubbish because the Snozzy's uniform they gave me was a recycled number.

"Watch that ankle," she said before I left.

I congratulated myself. I had been fiendishly clever, had fooled the SS. It would be the end of me and Brian and the end of the Two Peas. Good riddance. I would miss none of them.

The rain had stopped. I limped over to the playground. After a while I didn't feel so cunning and clever. I felt rotten, if you want to know the truth, rotten and phony, just like everyone and everything I hated.

So that night when the house was asleep I grabbed my cane and let myself out, telling myself it was for a stretch on the monkey ladder, but I really knew different, I knew exactly where I was going, and soon found myself in the school grounds. It was a bit dodgy getting my wrecked ankle through the gap under the fence, but I dragged it behind me, limped to the edge of the grave, and stood sweating and pondering in the darkness, waiting for the grave to grab me. This time I wanted to go for good: if I could find the Monaghans I wanted to stay with them; I could grit my teeth and endure the pains just so long as I never came back to rotten phony old Liverpool ever again.

My ankle throbbed. I felt a pull. I dropped the cane into the grave and clenched my fists. Then I closed my eyes and felt myself being lifted and hurled quickly into darkness.

. . . the faeries, with the power
of life and death over us

Free fall, weightless in the dark, and I knew it was happening again. Green light and the gatekeeper's smoldering eyes as he raised his lantern high to check me. I almost peed my pants with fright.

And then darkness and falling and the pains hit me. Not the ankle, but everything else.

Aftershock.

There was no mistaking that by-now-familiar burning sensation as every cell in my bodily universe was plunged into deep-fried hell; I clenched my teeth and howled, tears streaming down my face. Doubled up with the pain for the longest time, I knew I had to hang in and wait it out.

After it was over, after all the mollies had rezipped themselves, I lay on my back until my heart had stopped its pounding and I could unlock my jaw and breathe normally. Then I sat up and could see I was in a dark, gloomy room sitting on an old mattress. I tasted blood; I'd bitten my tongue.

But pain didn't matter. I was chuffed to be back. Chuffed was an understatement; delighted would be better, or blissed out. I'd made it. I was in a room with several people in it sleeping on smelly old mattresses, bedding, bundles of clothing. A glimmer of gray daylight filtered in through a window. There was no furniture of any kind in the room. I felt about for my cane but then remembered I'd thrown it into the grave. Holding on to the wall, I stood on my good foot. The botched one seemed normal. I reached down in the dark and felt the ankle with my fingers. The swelling had gone. I wiggled my foot about, leaned my weight on it: no pain. Rejuvenated mollies. Cured! As with the blow on the head from the soldier's billy club, my mollies had ignored the injury.

A good start. Now what? The Monaghans. I took a deep breath. The place smelled of sweat and body odor and mildew. I took a closer look at the only light source, a filthy window that hadn't been cleaned in years, and outside there was a well with an iron grating in the pavement above. I was in a cellar of some kind, a squatter's place probably, in a city. I knew something about squatting; you might say I was an expert. I bent and peered at the sleepers in the cellar. I counted four bundles of rags-and-bones, including two small kids, all asleep, or sick, or dying, I couldn't tell which. They didn't smell so good. There were no Monaghans.

I opened the only door and was on the outside in fresher air standing at the foot of several stone steps that ascended to the street above. I climbed the steps, relieved at the strength in my ankle, and looked about me. An old part of a city. It had been raining. Instead of the street being asphalt there were cobblestones glistening wet in the fading light, and muddy puddles, and it was windy and cold, not a bit like the warm September I'd left, but more like winter. People in old-fashioned clothes. They looked poor. The women wore long coats, worn and shabby, and little bitty hats or bonnets, and the men wore jackets and cloth caps. There were no cars, only horses and carts and carriages. The street had tall decaying terrace houses all the way as far along as I could see, many with broken windows, all with cellars like mine, and scruffy-looking front doors. The door above my basement had once had a number 11 attached to it above its letter box but the numerals had been removed, leaving only their outline on the peeling paintwork.

I walked to the end of the street and looked up at the sign: Paradise Street. The cross street was Hanover, cobblestoned, noisily busy, people hurrying, not all of them poor in this section, some well dressed, with chimney-pot hats, heavy coats, carrying umbrellas, and stepping daintily through horse manure as they crossed the street. A clattering commotion of horses and carts, horse-drawn carriages with well-dressed women and kids inside, the pong of horse dung poisoning the cold air. Beggars sitting cross-legged outside many of the shops, hands out or hats or caps in front of them on the sidewalk, most of the shops run-down and empty.

As I stared at the people I couldn't help thinking they were all dead now, every one of them, *now* being my own time. But it was probably still 1847—I'd have to ask someone—and they were all alive, living as though they didn't know they'd soon be dead. It was weird: I thought of millions of people living and dying, and always there were new people coming, who lived and died, and then more new people who lived and died, and so on for ever and ever, world without end, Amen.

It felt good to be walking normally, without a cane. I wandered along Hanover, which led into Canning—wider and noisier, with more beggars—and down to a river where a couple of high-masted sailing ships were being unloaded onto the docks and where the smells of creosote and tar and the sea replaced the stink of horse dung.

I was probably in Dublin. There was one way to find out: I asked a bloke in a bowler hat, "What city is this?" but he only snarled something at me and hurried off. I stopped a stout lady moving along in her wide, swishing skirts, like a ship under full sail. "City?" she said, surprised. "Why, it's Liverpool, of course, ducky, where else could it be?" She laughed and started to walk away, but I stopped her with another question. "What's the date today?"

"Monday the thirteenth, luv."

"Thirteenth of what?"

She looked surprised again. "March."

"What year?"

She began to look nervous. "Forty-eight," she said, hurrying away from me before I could ask her what century, clutching her purse, convinced by now that I was a mad criminal.

Liverpool in 1848; probable (who could be sure?) city of my birth, foreign and unrecognizable; even the street names had meant nothing, though I didn't know the downtown so well, the Old Swan I came from being several miles off to the east.

I began to figure it out: it was about four months since I'd seen the Monaghans in Westport. They must have made it to Dublin, and from there they had sailed across the Irish Sea to Liverpool. Why else would the grave or the gatekeeper or the faeries, with the power of life and death over us, have deposited me here?

And the place I'd landed in was probably important, too: Paradise Street. I turned my back on the docks and traipsed back up the hill, taking a shortcut through the mean narrow streets; avoiding the puddles of filth and the heaps of smelly rubbish, through the squash of people and past alleys and cellars crowded with starving, sick people, heading in the direction of the squatters' cellar.

I looked in some of the other cellars along the way and saw dying people, all Irish immigrants by the sound of them, their swollen faces black with disease, limbs puffed up like balloons, a few of them like raving lunatics, twitching and shouting and screaming. The smell was the worst; I held my nose and retreated back up the steps.

I was a bit dizzy, like I'd downed a bottle of beer too fast.

The tingling I'd had in my hands and fingers the first time, in Achill, wasn't there, but I had a funny kind of feeling of looseness, of not being all together, of disintegration, like some of my mollies were late arriving, were temporarily misplaced in never-never land and hadn't shown up yet. I longed to lie down and sleep.

The light was dim in the Paradise Street cellar. The only person awake, a woman, sat on a mattress, her back against the wall. Two very young girls, covered with a ragged blanket, slept beside her. I threw myself down on a vacant mattress leaking its stuffing, covered myself with a rag of blanket, and went out like a light.

I don't know how long I slept, but woke with a start when the door banged open. I sat up. The cellar was full of shadows. A lighted stub of candle burned steadily on a wooden packing crate.

"God save all here!"

Tully Monaghan.

He hadn't seen me. I stared at him, framed in the shadowed doorway, the ragged clothes too big for his slight frame, but it was the same Tully I remembered. Seeing him there, I felt a huge surge of happy satisfaction: Hannah could not be far behind.

. . . the noblest work of god

How is my mother, Alice?" Tully Monaghan asked the woman with the two girls.

"She's no better," the woman said, glancing across the floor at one of the sleepers.

Tully kneeled. He held a bottle of milk in his hand. I could see now that the bundle in the corner was Maggie Monaghan, wasted and sick beyond recognition. "It's me, Ma." Tully ripped the top off the bottle of milk.

"Let me." It was Hannah, suddenly there, kneeling beside her mother. I hadn't seen her come in. A wild bursting in my heart at the sight of her.

Tully lifted his mother to a sitting position and held her

while Hannah fed her milk from the bottle, slowly and patiently so the milk didn't dribble down her chin, talking to her in a low murmur. Ma didn't take much. Then Tully laid her gently down. Hannah put the still-almost-full bottle on the crate beside the candle.

I watched them, unwilling to reveal myself, for I was chuffed beyond belief at the sight and sound of them, and I didn't want it to stop.

Tully gasped when he saw me. "Lord save us!" he said, backing off and making a hurried sign of the cross. Hannah turned and saw me, and rushed and threw her arms around me. "Oh, Tom!"

Tully stared at me like I wasn't real, the old fear and suspicion back in his eyes.

Hannah was so excited she could hardly speak. "How did you find us?"

I stood back, holding her hands, studying her in the candlelight. Thinner, paler, weaker, her clothes little more than rags, though still the same Hannah, bursting with feeling. She was wearing what looked to be a man's jacket, too big for her, sleeves turned up in a cuff. Her hands, usually so white and clean, were dirty. She wore a ring. I ran my thumb over the heart and hands and the crown.

She smiled. "The ring is on the left hand, see?" She held it up. "Worn on the right hand means a girl has not yet found her true love, but on the left . . ." She stopped. "I knew you'd come back, Tom."

Tully, recovered, fear and suspicion gone, or masked, said,

"It's good to see you, Tom." He wore the same heavy twill trousers as before, but with a heavy gray shirt.

"I'm *so* happy to see you!" cried Hannah, throwing herself at me.

Tully took my hand and shook it. Hannah hugged me again and then she hugged Tully. Tully grinned. "Easy! Easy, girl, or you'll have us destroyed for the want of air."

When Hannah had calmed down a bit I asked, "Where's Brendan?"

"He will be here shortly," she said. "He is out fetching water and finding blankets for new immigrants, those with small childer. He's good with the little ones. They'd do anything he asked."

They filled me in on their journey to Liverpool. Clancy's men had tried to stop them, but the Monaghans had made so much noise hammering on the sides of the cart and screaming like banshees that the horse had bolted through their ranks. They had crossed the country to Dublin in practically no time at all. "Ah! You would never believe the sad sights we've seen," sighed Tully. They had been lucky to get on a ship transporting cows and pigs and grain to Liverpool—food needed by the starving Irish, Tully said angrily—and needing ballast, which meant they had traveled free, along with hundreds of others escaping famine and disease. Since then they had been haunting the Liverpool docks every day for the past two months, looking for a ship to take them as ballast to America, but had met no luck so far.

Brendan came in and sank down on the floor, exhausted,

back against the wall. He didn't notice me. I was surprised at how happy I felt to see him.

"Hello, Brendan," I said. "Do you remember me?"

He looked up, gaped, struggled to his feet. "Tom!" His tired face melted into a smile. "Keeya! Hey, Tom? Keeya!" He clasped me in a bear hug.

I asked Hannah and Tully about Ma and they immediately became solemn.

"We worry about her," said Hannah. "She gets no better."

"Ma gets no better," repeated Brendan sorrowfully.

"I swear I will never puzzle you out, Tom Mullen," said Hannah, "showing up at the oddest times and disappearing like the sun at day's end. The last I saw of you was your back in the darkness, and the sky full of stars."

Tully said, "We've done nothing but talk about you all these weeks. You saved our lives with the fine horse and rig. We would have been lost without it, and so would many others we picked up along the way."

"Did you sell the horse and cart in Dublin?"

"Ah, no," said Tully. "We met an Achill man in Dublin who took the noble animal and promised to bring more hungry souls out from the west."

Hannah said, "We owe you our lives, Tom."

"None of you will last much longer unless we get food into you," I said. "And a doctor for your mother."

"Haven't I tried," said Tully. "But the doctors stay away from the poor, terrified they'll catch the fever."

"And there's no money for food," said Hannah.

I searched their faces. They didn't have a clue. Babes in the wood. They were in a city full of food and they didn't know how to get it. But stealing was alien to the Monaghans; they'd never begged and they'd never stolen. Yet there was one thing I was certain of: without food they'd die.

They needed me again.

The cellar was a stinker, but, delighted to be back—no "Jingle Bells"—I slept soundly that night.

Awakened early by the grind and rattle of cartwheels on the cobbled street outside, I sat up and rubbed my eyes. The air in the cellar was poisonously thick and hot.

"I've got to get out," I said to Tully. Hannah and Brendan were still asleep beside their mother.

"Then I'll come with you. You're like a leprechaun, Tom Mullen; if you follow the tricky little shoemaker to his pot of gold but let him out of your sight for an instant, then he's gone forever."

"Problem is I've got no pot of gold, Tully."

I was happy to see Tully's friendliness was back to where it had been after the Champion of Mayo fight.

"You're not leaving us already, Tom?" Hannah awake.

"I need fresh air, that's all."

"I'll go with him," said Tully, "and make sure he gets in no trouble. Will you stay with Ma?"

"I will," said Hannah, "but don't be long or I'll start worrying about you. I never saw such a wild and dangerous place, with horses and carriages charging down on you, and all manner of beggars and ferocious vagabonds."

Outside, the morning light glimmered bleakly through thin fog the color and smell of horse dung, but it was preferable to the cellar's toxic fug. We set off along the street, busy already with carriages and carts coming and going, and I could see dimly through the murk the shapes of people moving about their business. Untidy spills of humanity slept huddled together for warmth in the doorways of abandoned shops.

We came to a stable yard busy with men and draft horses; there was a blacksmith's shop with one man pumping a bellows at a burning red furnace and a second man sweating over the hammering and shaping of horseshoes. We stood and watched them for a minute, the whoosh of the bellows and the high ringing sounds of hammer on anvil like music. I noticed a pile of leather horse tackle in the yard and a rack of nose bags, the kind used for horse feed. When no one was looking I slipped one of the sacks off the rack and tucked it under my arm. "Let's go," I said to Tully.

"What do you want with the feed bag?"

"Food," I said as we walked quickly along.

Tully smiled. "You have money, Tom?"

"Carry this." I gave him the sack. Good grief! He was like a baby. You'd never think I was more than two years younger. We came to a fruit and vegetable market in the cobbled square, huge it was, with like, what, forty or fifty stalls and handcarts? Selling everything from apples—though many of them were discolored or rotten—to fish. The market was busy and foggy enough for me to nick a few things easily without being noticed. "Follow me," I said to Tully.

It was too easy. There were so many people crowded around the stalls that all I had to do was reach in between the press of people and help myself to an apple here, a bunch of carrots there, and drop them into Tully's bag. We weren't the only ones nicking stuff either, with snotty-nosed kids all over the place, dodging in and out like flies, grabbing and running as fast as their bare feet would go over the greasy cobblestones. Pretty soon our bag was half full. Tully, hanging on to the bag, looked ill, like he was about to keel over. "That should do for now, Tully," I said, anxious to get away before he collapsed.

We were no sooner away from the market, on the way back to Paradise, when Tully stopped and leaned weakly against the wall. I took the bag from him. "You okay?"

He slid down the wall and sat on the ground. "I'm trembling so much I can't go on."

The fever! "Are you sick?"

"Not sick. Just frightened to death."

"There's nothing to be frightened of, Tully."

"I never stole a thing in my life. God will never forgive us, Tom, for the terrible sin. I couldn't believe my eyes when I saw you taking all that . . . food, I swear to God. I was terrified we'd be caught and hanged."

"It's only a bit of food, Tully."

Tully said, "It's a sin."

"Sin is for rich people, Tully, not for us. We can't afford it."

I couldn't believe that this was the same wild, sarcastic Tully from Achill, Irish rebel, drinker of poteen, whining now about sin . . .

"But it's not honest, Tom, there's the rub of it. 'An honest man is the noblest work of God'—my da drummed that into us."

. . . the same fearless boy who fished in his cockleshell boat in the middle of a storm and fought soldiers on horses?

"Do you remember, Tully, how you told me to drink your poteen like a man? And how you sneered when I refused? Well, I don't know what a man is, Tully, but I don't think it has anything to do with strong drink. Maybe it's got more to do with strong purpose, knowing how to take care of yourself and your family, even if you have to steal for them. Come on, get up before the police see us." I grabbed his arm and helped him to his feet, and then we fled along a narrow alley, filthy with human waste and horse dung.

Hannah woke me and Tully up. "Brendan is still out. I'm worried something has happened to him." She lit the candle.

The cellar was quiet. I guessed it to be about midnight or one o'clock. We crawled out of our makeshift beds.

Tully said to Hannah, "He'll be all right, don't worry. Probably lost his way. The streets confuse him. You stay here with Ma while Tom and I go out and find him. Tom, will you search the low roads if I take the high?"

The night was raw, with a biting wind; I zipped up my jacket to the chin and walked quickly, threading my way back and forth through the quiet, deserted streets that led down to the docks.

After searching for about an hour, just when I'd decided I

would never find him I spotted his dark bulk ahead of me in the street. I was sure it was him. "Brendan!" I shouted.

He turned and waited. I ran to him. His tired face lit up at the sight of me. "Tom!" was all he could say.

"Brendan," I said.

"I was lost, Tom."

"I know, Brendan." He was carrying something. "What have you got?"

"Only blankets, Tom."

His arms were hooked through a bundle of old empty sacks, hessians and twills, the kind used for grain, but torn or damaged, discards. I remembered Hannah saying something about Brendan helping new immigrants.

"Where did you get them from?" I asked him.

He couldn't point because his arms were full. Instead he nodded his head toward the docks. "There's heaps and heaps of them, Tom, down by the ships."

"Let's go, Brendan. Tully and Hannah are worried about you."

"They're for the childer, Tom, to keep warm. But I couldn't find my way back."

"That's okay, Brendan, I know the way. You want me to carry some of those for you?"

"I can carry the blankets, Tom. They're not heavy."

I looked at his face in the light of a streetlamp and could see that he had been crying.

Poor lost Brendan. He broke me up, he really did.

. . . taking care of yourself against the bullies of the world

A flood of Irish immigrants arrived on a ship from Dublin that same morning and our cellar became crowded, with more than a dozen people in it. The food we'd nicked wasn't enough for everyone. Three of the newcomers were men who set off to find food for themselves and their families. The problem of water was solved by filling an old bucket and a kettle from a horse trough pump on Hanover Street. There was no lavatory; people went out at night and used the alley or a small patch of waste ground.

Maggie Monaghan couldn't eat.

Brendan had stomach pains after eating an apple and broke out in a sweat.

Brendan was sick. Not just a stomachache from a bad apple but something more serious. His eyes shone like high-beam headlights.

"Your ma is not the only one who needs a doctor," I murmured to Tully.

"He has caught something from the sick immigrants," said Hannah. "We've got to find a doctor."

"I'll come with you," I said.

Hannah said, "Tully will stay with Ma and Brendan."

We legged it up the hill, into a posher district, where even the weather seemed better, with cleaner air, and with normal shops and houses, and people in fine clothes riding in fine carriages.

We peered at the signs on the shops and houses until we came to a big house with a brass plate on the door: Dr. Crispin Beddoes, Physician. Hannah raised the heavy iron knocker and let it fall three times. A woman opened the door and frowned when she saw us standing on the step. "What do you want?" Black dress, white pinafore, starched white bonnet.

"My ma is sick, ma'am," said Hannah. "Could the good doctor—"

"The doctor is out." The woman closed the door firmly.

The same thing happened on Brownlow Hill, and on Rodney Street.

"It's no good, Tom," Hannah sighed, the breeze tossing her hair about. "They'll not come. There's too much talk of the Irish famine fever spreading." She shook her head. "The good

Dr. Adams himself was struck down in Achill, God rest his soul, just before we set out, and there's no cure for it. The doctors have a right to be fearful, for it is swamping Liverpool. It doesn't seem to matter whether you catch the black fever or the yellow, for they both carry you off. Didn't I see a cart loaded with dead souls yesterday making for the country, covered with a canvas, but there was no doubt what was in it."

Brendan and the mother were sleeping when we got back. Ma looked like she wouldn't last another night. Brendan seemed a bit brighter. Tully had covered them with a few of Brendan's sacks, though the cellar was warm with the press of so many people, some sitting with their backs against the walls, staring into space, but most of them stretched out on bedding, asleep or resting. I wondered if Brendan and Ma might not be better off sleeping in the doorway of some abandoned shop where at least the air, if you didn't mind the smell of horse dung, would be fresher than the awful pong of unwashed bodies and foul breath.

Tully peeled an orange and Brendan ate it, along with small amounts of raw turnip and parsnip. Ma would eat nothing. "It's meat they need," said Tully.

That night, Hannah stayed behind and Tully and I nipped up the hill to the posh district and stopped at a restaurant window and stared in at the well-dressed people eating dinner and drinking wine. It was cold outside. Tully was shivering.

"Lots of nice meat in there," I said, "and it's already cooked."

Tully's eyes were staring. "That's all very well, but—"

"Come on." I pushed through the door and marched into

the restaurant, Tully behind me. All the fine ladies and gentlemen stared. A fat man with a red face called loudly, "Waiter!" I grabbed a whole roast chicken off his plate and ran for the door.

A waiter stood at the door barring my way. Then another. They looked mean. I had the chicken in my two hands as they converged on me. "Catch, Tully," I yelled, throwing the chicken at him. He caught it. The waiters stopped. Tully ran for the door, but they moved swiftly to cut him off. I ran behind them and Tully threw the chicken over their heads and I caught it and fled out the door, not waiting to see if Tully had made it. When I had run thirty yards with no one behind me I stopped and looked back and saw the two waiters pitching him out into the muddy street. One of them put his boot in, but Tully scrambled to his feet and ran.

"You okay?" I asked him.

He laughed. "I'm fine, Tom, but I know now for sure that it was the Devil himself sent you to us." He laughed again and rubbed his muddy thigh where the waiter had kicked him. "That was the great lark, so it was."

We headed back to the cellar. "I've been thinking," said Tully, "about that fighting of yours, the skipping and the leaping and the acrobatics and all, the way you downed the Champion of Mayo."

"Yeah?"

"Do you think I would be able to learn that?"

I shrugged. "I don't see why not."

"I've been thinking over what you said about taking care of

myself and my family, and you're right. Taking care of yourself against the bullies of the world is important, right?"

"Right."

"Then you'll teach me, Tom?"

"We can start tomorrow."

We carried the chicken back to the cellar like it was a prize we'd won in battle, and Brendan ate a little of it. Ma could eat none. The old lady didn't look good; her face was the yellow-white color of parsnips and slicked with sweat. We ate a bit, then gave the rest of the chicken to Alice for her two kids.

By this time most of the Irish immigrants had left our cellar, finding places less crowded. The few that remained drank each night a cheap Liverpool swill called swipes, made from the sour rinsings from beer barrels and bought at the dockside for a few pennies a bucket. Tully took a mouthful and immediately spat it out.

I wandered up the hill one night and found an overcoat thrown over the wall of a posh house. Worn at the neck and cuffs but with no rips or tears, it was thick and warm and would keep Tully from shivering. I carried it back and he tried it on. It was brown and straight and encircled him like a tube. "Looks like it was made for you," I said.

"It's a lovely coat, Tully," said Hannah, admiring the material. "And it suits you well." She smiled. "You look like a toff, doesn't he, Brendan?"

"You look like a toff, Tully," said Brendan. He seemed stronger.

"You're sure it's not stolen?" Tully asked me suspiciously.

"Would I lie to you, Tully?"

"You would. But it's the grand coat. Thank you kindly, Tom, but are you sure you don't need it for yourself?"

"My jacket is warm." I could see that he liked the coat, but could see also that his mind was somewhere else. He looked worried.

"What's up?"

"Ma gets no better."

But she did get a bit better, sitting up and drinking milk and chewing on small pieces of carrot.

Hannah hardly ever left her side.

Tully took to kung fu like an eagle to the air.

We practiced in a deserted alleyway for a couple of hours each day, and, like Lanny, I gave him homework, things to practice on his own. I even told him about some of the other kung fu stuff I remembered that Lanny said was important, stuff like "Claim no possessions so that none may claim you" and "The coward and the hero march together in every man" and "A wise man does not contend; yield and overcome." Tully liked that stuff, I could tell, because he always wanted to discuss with me and Hannah afterward what it meant.

And I tried to teach him how to nick stuff without getting caught, but he worried too much about sin and hell and the shee-og and stuff like that.

————

Hannah didn't like us stealing either.

When she found out she was horrified. "You're the terrible pair of sinners!"

"Struggling to survive is not a sin, Hannah," I argued.

" 'Thou shalt not steal.' It's the sixth commandment," she said angrily.

"Seventh," said Tully.

"The seventh is adultery," argued Hannah.

"That's the sixth."

"That's what I said in the first place," said Hannah. She had another thought. "We will all end up in prison! Do you know the penalty for stealing?"

I shrugged.

"God forgive us our sins," said Hannah.

"Amen," said Tully solemnly.

. . . a fine house with bay windows and calico curtains

"Will you just look at that!" said Hannah.

I followed her awed glance. We were sitting on the steps of a shop in the posh district up the hill, eating a couple of apples I'd nicked, while across the street two women in rich, colorful dresses and feathery hats were alighting from a black carriage. The coachman looked down from his high perch while a footman held the door open and the women hiked their dresses up over their ankles, stepped down daintily, and disappeared into a ladies' dress shop.

Hannah said, "Did you ever lay eyes on such grand clothes and carriages? And such grand people?" She finished her apple. I took the core and threw it into a pile of fresh manure in the middle of the street. "Stolen apple," she said. "Isn't it a wonder it didn't choke me?"

For an answer I threw my core after Hannah's, to be churned up under the hooves of horses.

We had been knocking on the doors of the medical houses all morning, searching for a doctor to come to Ma, but it had been a waste of time; no one would come. Hannah was tired; there were dark circles under her eyes. I looked at her pinched white face and her skinny little body lost in the man's jacket with its elbows out and upturned cuffs, and I worried that she might be the next to catch the dreadful fever that was killing so many.

The fancy ladies emerged from the shop.

"That'll be me someday," said Hannah, her nose in the air. "Dressed in fine linens and long silken gowns and fine petticoats that flounce to the ground, and smart bonnets, with my own horse and carriage and my own coachman to drive me to the shops. And I will always give money to help the poor. What do you think of that?"

Without waiting for an answer, she went on, "Or perhaps I'll be a doctor, a brilliant doctor, renowned throughout the land for my cures, who always comes when called, no matter how rich or poor the people are, no matter how sick they are."

She paused, thinking. Then she said, "And I will live in a fine house with bay windows and calico curtains, and a dog."

We walked back down the hill to our cellar in the slums.

Brendan was sick again. He could eat nothing. Anything he swallowed came back.

His skin was yellow.

And Maggie's improvement had been only temporary. She was back to refusing food and sleeping all the time.

Like his mother, all Brendan wanted to do was sleep. I felt his forehead; it was hot and sweaty. "Keeya, Tom," he murmured.

"Keeya, Brendan," I said. "You've got to get well."

"We're brothers, Tom, me and you and Tully, right?"

"That's right, Brendan, brothers. Get well, okay?"

He smiled and slept.

"What about a hospital?" I said to Tully as the idea hit me. "If we took Brendan and your mother they would have to treat them, wouldn't they?"

"Where is it, the hospital, and how would we get them there?"

"Come on, let's find out."

We headed over to Hanover and asked a pair of local women talking together outside a pub if they knew if there was a hospital. There was the workhouse fever ward, they said, not far away, and pointed up the hill toward Mount Pleasant.

"We need a handcart," I said to Tully, and led the way to the market, where we borrowed an empty cart, brushing off dirt and withered cabbage leaves with our feet and hands. The cart had iron-rimmed wheels that rattled and clattered on the cobbles as we hurried back to the cellar.

We dragged an old mattress out and up the steps and threw it in the cart. Then the three of us carried Ma, weightless as a bamboo chair, and Brendan up from the cellar and laid them on the mattress. Brendan woke. "Hannah?" he muttered deliriously.

The short journey up the hill wasn't an easy one, even with the three of us pushing, but we eventually made it into the front yard of the workhouse, a large two-story plain brick building.

The place was chaos. A small crowd of sick people was blocking the door, trying to get in. Me and Hannah stayed with the cart, standing and watching, while Tully stitched himself through the crowd and in through the workhouse door. He was out again within a few minutes. "There isn't a bed to be had," he said. "They're putting people out in sheds and tents on the grass out back. It's like the Battle of the Boyne in there, nurses rushing about and people crying and moaning like banshees. They said they will get to us as soon as they can; we will have to be patient."

We waited. Hannah stroked her mother's brow and sang a slow sad song quietly in Irish.

After a while a nurse came out to inspect the sick. With her were helpers with stretchers. The worst cases were to be taken into one of the sheds or tents. She examined Ma and Brendan. "Your mother and brother, you say?" she asked Tully.

"Yes, ma'am."

"Names?"

"Maggie and Brendan Monaghan."

"And your names?"

"Tully Monaghan, ma'am. And Hannah and Tom."

Tom what? Monaghan? The name felt good on me, like a comfortable pair of shoes.

"Tent five," she told the stretcher bearers. We followed the stretchers round the back of the workhouse into a long canvas tent where about fifty people were lying on bedding laid on the grass and spaced along the tent walls. Not one person moved; they looked like they were dead. There was only one nurse in the tent. The tent was cold.

We saw Maggie and Brendan settled. "Dr. Watterson will examine them later," the nurse told Tully. She was very young, probably about the same age as Tully; she looked tired.

"What do you think, yourself?" Hannah asked the nurse. "Is it the fever they have?"

The nurse shook her head and hurried away before we could ask anything more.

We pushed the handcart back to the market, but instead of returning to the Paradise Street cellar we trekked back up the hill, found an empty shop with a broken window on Ainsworth Street, near the workhouse, and spent the night inside in a dirty but empty back room.

The next morning we went to the tent behind the workhouse. There were even more people than the day before, many of them camped out on the grounds, most of them sick.

Ma Monaghan was sleeping. Her face was lemon-pie yellow. A young Irish nurse, a different one from the previous day, told us that Ma had been vomiting in the night. "I'm afraid it's the fever she has, right enough," she said sadly.

"And Brendan?" asked Hannah in a whisper.

The young nurse shrugged helplessly.

Hannah sniffed, trying not to cry.

"What are their chances?" asked Tully.

"Normally your mother might have a chance, but her poor body is weak and malnourished," said the nurse. "I wouldn't have your hopes too high. Your brother is stronger. He might make it." She looked about her at the other patients. "It's the Irish famine fever. They all have it, God help them."

Brendan woke at the sound of our voices and struggled to sit up. The nurse made him lie back. We kneeled on the ground beside him. Hannah held his hand. His yellowed face glistened with sweat. He couldn't speak. He closed his eyes and slept. The nurse brought a bowl of cold water and a cloth and sponged his forehead.

"Let me," said Hannah, releasing Brendan's hand and taking the cloth and cooling her brother's face and neck with gentle dabs.

We stayed all afternoon while Ma and Brendan slept.

. . . like a wounded bird

Tully got over his fear and dread of stealing food and became as good as me at nicking stuff, though we had to run for it once or twice when he wasn't fast enough and the shopkeeper copped him at it. One shopkeeper grabbed his arm and wouldn't let go. "Fetch a bobby!" he yelled to people passing in the street.

"Let him go, mister," I said. "We're hungry."

"Police! Police!" the man yelled, his fat face boiling with excitement.

I gave him a light kick on the shin, enough to make him hop about on one leg. But he still held on grimly to Tully. Tully kicked his other shin and he was free. "Keeya!" he yelled.

"We're not doing anyone a bit of harm, Tom," Tully said afterward, "and it's small excitement for us in this terrible cold city that makes the committing of sins so necessary."

He often called the city cold. It had no heart, he said. Thousands of poor starving Irish wretches living in cold, overcrowded cellars or doorways without the helping hand of charity. "There's only free transportation to a pauper's grave when all the suffering is over," he said.

There was good news: Brendan seemed to be mending, sitting up weakly in the fever tent and talking a bit, and we began to hope. But Ma was still the same.

"Remember you once said I was pretty, Tom?" Hannah said sadly one afternoon as she saw her reflection in a shop window mirror, up the hill in the posh area. "Well, now I look a sorry sight, more like a scarecrow."

"You're still the prettiest girl in all of Ireland."

"Will you come with us to America, Tom, once we find a ship?"

"If you want me."

"Of course I want you. And Tully needs you. Remember the shooting star and our wishes?"

"Yes, Hannah. You made three."

"I made four. You were in my star wish, but I didn't tell you."

She put her arm through mine and we walked through the busy streets and it felt nice walking with Hannah like that, though I'd never do such a thing in Old Swan, not even with Hannah; she was, after all, a girl.

We had made our back room on Ainsworth a little more comfortable for sleeping, with cushions and blankets nicked from a posh carriage, and had swept the debris off the floor. Tully continued to go to the docks every day, looking for a ship that would take Irish emigrants as ballast, but he'd had no luck. If only we could get to America everything would be all right, he said over and over. There was no money to pay for our passage. It would cost at least four or five pounds, six months' wages for a working man, he told me, to sail to America. Unless we could get taken as ballast we hadn't a chance of getting out of Liverpool.

I resolved to nick some money from one of the big houses on the hill, for Hannah and Tully. I didn't think, somehow, that Brendan and Ma would be going, and I had a feeling that I wouldn't be going with them either.

Brendan got bad again, worse than before, taking on the same parsnip color of his mother, vomiting, and then sleeping. The doctor shrugged sadly whenever Tully asked him if he could save his brother. "It's the relapsing fever," he said. They were all doing their best, he said.

Hannah, as affectionate as ever, but no longer eager and happy as she had been in Achill, was like a wounded bird. She watched over her ma and Brendan and had little to say. I remembered the old Hannah, bursting with life. What a waste. Nothing made sense; the whole universe was phony.

The next day the young Irish nurse met us at the tent entrance. She said to Tully, "Your poor mother was too far gone. She passed away in the night. Father Grogan gave her the last rites." She laid a hand on his arm. "She is in heaven this very minute, resting in the loving arms of Jesus."

Hannah cried quietly in Tully's arms.

Tully said to the nurse, "Could we see her?"

The nurse led them away to the workhouse building. I waited outside the tent.

When they came back their eyes were red from weeping.

We took a look at Brendan. He was asleep.

Hannah stroked his brow and his eyelids fluttered open. "Hannah?" The blue of his eyes, swamped by enlarged pupils, was almost colorless against his yellow skin. "Hannah?"

"I'm here, Brendan, right beside you. Here's my hand."

"I can't see you!"

"Listen to me, Brendan," Hannah whispered desperately. "You've got to get well. D'you hear?"

"Hannah?" He struggled to speak. "Will you stay with me, Hannah?"

"Of course I will, Brendan. I'll be here. I won't go away."

"And Ma? And Tully?"

"I'm here, Brendan." Tully gripped Brendan's shoulder. "Ma is fine, don't worry."

"And Tom?"

"He's here, too," said Hannah.

I stepped forward. "Hello, Brendan. It's me, Tom."

"Tom . . ."

He closed his eyes and his pale lips curved in a smile. After a while I got up and went away.

The next night, after sitting on the grass most of the day with Hannah and Tully at Brendan's bedside, after watching Hannah's thin white face and sad eyes, I walked the streets until my legs ached, fists pushed down inside the pockets of my jacket. I eventually found myself at the waterfront. The air was bitterly cold. Except for the groans of ropes and rigging it was quiet; there was no one about. Nothing moved except the reflections from a ship's lantern shimmering in the black water. I could see the lights of Seacombe and Birkenhead on the other side of the river.

Brendan was dying, I just knew it.

Brendan who never harmed anybody. No sense. Nothing made sense.

I didn't want to be around in 1848 when it happened, didn't want to watch poor old Brendan wasting away to . . . nothing. When I had been clutched into the grave two weeks ago I'd wanted to stay with the Monaghans and never go back ever again to Old Swan or the Two Peas or Brian, but now I couldn't watch Brendan dying. It was twisting me up. I remembered Mrs. Feinberg. Watching her. Waiting. This was the same. I wanted out.

I climbed over a dock gate with sharp bits on the top that made my goolies shrink with worry when I had only the one leg over, and walked out to the end of the slip and looked down at the black water twenty feet below. This was the same river Mersey I'd crossed many times on the ferry from the Pier

Head to explore Birkenhead or New Brighton on the opposite shore, ducking under the turnstile so I wouldn't have to buy a ticket. It was a place common to both centuries. Jumping into its ice-cold water would be sure to shock my mollies into return flight—after all, if a fall into a scalpeen could do it . . .

It was dark, with no moon, and cold, with the March wind cutting in off the river. I closed my eyes. This time I was going for good; there was no coming back. I clenched my fists. "Goodbye, Hannah," I called out as I jumped . . .

I knew almost right away that it was no good because I splashed down in the water instead of falling into the gatekeeper's dark limbo.

So I had to swim for it, dragging myself up the ladder on the side of the dock like the creature from the black lagoon, the weight of my wet clothes dragging me back. Then I had to trudge all the way back up the hill to Ainsworth, sopping-wet and shivering with the cold.

I stepped carefully through the broken window and into the back of the shop. Hannah and Tully were out.

I trudged up to Mount Pleasant and found them at Brendan's bedside, Tully fast asleep on the ground with his mouth open. Hannah didn't ask me why I was sopping wet, didn't even notice. Brendan was unconscious.

I sat beside Hannah. "How is he?"

She shook her head.

I put my arm around her and she leaned her head on my wet shoulder like a little kid of five.

Hannah noticed my wet clothes. "Did you fall into a horse trough?"

"I fell in the river."

"Go in the back and take off your things. You can put on Tully's overcoat." Tully's coat was thrown over the foot of the bed.

I stripped off in the workhouse lavatory and put on the coat. Why hadn't I taken off my jacket before I jumped? There were no washers and dryers in 1848. I had only Tully's overcoat to wear until my togs dried outside in the March wind.

I sat with Hannah at the bedside, naked under Tully's coat, Hannah holding Brendan's hand and talking quietly to him, letting him know we were there, but if he heard anything you'd never know it.

You don't want to know how he looked.

I dozed off and woke just before dawn. Hannah and Tully were asleep.

Brendan lay very still. I nudged Hannah awake. She put her ear to his chest and stayed there, her arms around her brother like she was sleeping, and then Tully woke and called the nurse and I saw that Hannah was weeping.

The Irish nurse whispered, "The boy slipped quietly away from us, without any pain or fuss. God rest him."

Tully kneeled and said a prayer. Hannah kneeled beside him, holding on to Brendan's hand, but she didn't pray.

A yolk-smear dawn was breaking over black rooftops as we trudged back to our squat, shoulders hunched against the cold wind. Hannah and Tully had only themselves now.

And me.

It was the worst time.

Hannah sat in the squat, dull-eyed, often tearful, refusing to come out, eating nothing. Tully couldn't help her because he had started acting crazy, coming and going without a word. He looked like a wild man, with burning eyes and grim mouth. I tried following him but he shook me off, losing me in a maze of foul alleys with names like Rotten Row, or disappearing in the crowds of filthy beggars, rag and rubbish-pickers, carts, and truck horses that thronged the dock road.

I pleaded with Hannah. "You've got to help each other now. Tully needs you." But talking did no good; it was like there was no one home.

The next day Tully woke late and when I asked him to let me help he growled angrily like a dog, then started to cry. It was the first time he had cried since his brother's death. I sat on the floor beside him, my arm round his shoulder. Then Hannah came and put her arm round his shoulder and cried with him.

After that they began to talk.

And eat. There was all this food I'd nicked. We ate some fruit while they talked of Brendan and Ma, letting it all hang out. They were more like their old selves, like the crying had mended some broken thing.

After they were all talked out, I decided to tell them everything. It seemed like the right time.

"Remember I said I fell in the river?"

They looked at me.

"I didn't fall in the river, I jumped."

"You jumped?" Tully.

"I was trying to get back home. I didn't want to stay any longer and see Brendan . . . die."

They thought about that for a while. Then Hannah said, "But isn't Liverpool your home?"

"It is, but . . ."

I told them everything, how I was from more than a century in the future, how the grave had called and taken me, everything. I wanted them to know because not telling them had been a kind of lie. I wanted them to know who I really was; telling them was the only thing left for me to do. I just had to do it, no matter what they thought.

When I was finished I searched their faces, trying to read their feelings, but what I saw on Tully's face made me almost wish I'd said nothing. I saw astonishment but I also saw that old fear and suspicion back in his eyes.

"Is it mad you are?" he said.

"Everything I've told you is true."

"I believe it, Tom," said Hannah. "I believe every word."

"You were sent to destroy us!" Tully moved away from me.

I said, "That's crap, Tully."

"First my da, then Ma, and now Brendan." Face cold and hard. Accusing.

"That's not it—"

"And we're to be the next, I suppose—"

"Tully! Will you stop!" Hannah cried. "Tom is telling the truth."

"I had nothing to do with their deaths, Tully, and you know it. Why I'm here I don't know. I think it was an accident if you really want to know the truth, something to do with being in the right or wrong place at the right or wrong time, I don't know, but I wasn't sent to destroy you. I've only ever wanted to help. You and Hannah and Brendan and your ma are like my real family, you've got to believe that."

He watched me for a minute in silence, thinking. Then he said, "It's true you saved our lives. But you've told us nothing about yourself."

"What could I say, Tully? 'I'm from the year 1974'? You wouldn't have believed me, just like you don't believe me now."

I saw him soften.

"Besides," I said, "except for you and Hannah I don't have any family. I'm alone."

"Is that the truth of it?" said Tully.

"Yes."

There was a short silence while Tully seemed to be considering things. Then he said slyly, "Tell me what it's like, this future of yours."

He was testing me, trying to catch me out in a lie. "It's . . . different . . . and the same." I stopped. How could I describe the future? Tell about television? Tell about huge international jets seven miles up in the sky, when the first flimsy airplane was still like, what, fifty or sixty years away? Describe cars? The traffic jams on Precky Road? High-speed motorways criss-crossing the country? The cinema? Rock music? What would they think of Pink Floyd's new album, *Dark Side of the Moon*? Or the new Rolling Stones' *Goat's Head Soup*? They wouldn't understand. In this world of theirs there were no typewriters or record players, no electric light; Alexander Graham Bell—I struggled to recall my *Science Facts*—was probably a snotty-nosed kid in Scotland; it would be another thirty years or so before he would invent the telephone. The first internal-combustion engine and the first radio were like, what, forty or fifty years in the future? I could tell them all this, but I didn't want to. Nor did I want to show them the few coins in my pocket with twentieth-century dates on them, I don't know why except I wanted them to believe me, to believe what I told them, to trust me. This was no game. Either they took my word for it or they didn't.

"It's mostly the same," I said. "New inventions, like the zipper on my jacket, and other things that if I told you about you'd say I was making up, but important things don't seem changed at all."

"Ah, the zipper! It's from the future, then." Tully.

I nodded.

Tully said, "The future. Ha! Brendan's death has addled all our heads, I think, but yours more than mine."

I said nothing. He didn't take his eyes off my face.

He said, "I've always thought there was something peculiar about you, Tom Mullen, but I put it down to you coming from England, foreign in ways and speech to the likes of simple Irish peasants." He paused, thinking. Then he said, "But let's just say it's true what you're after telling us. What good has it served? It's true you saved my life, but what of Da and Ma? And Brendan? With them gone we've nothing left."

"Don't be talking of nothing left," said Hannah. "We have each other, Tully."

"It was you and your family that brought me here," I said. "I believe that you were the magnet, Tully."

"Me and my family." Tully looked up, studying me, his eyes red. "Perhaps we're related. What do you say to that?"

"I think you could be my great-great-grandfather."

"You look so alike," said Hannah. "I'm not a bit surprised."

"Yes." I paused. "Even to birthmarks on our backsides."

Tully, his fear forgotten for the moment, frowned skeptically. "You're kidding me."

"It's the truth."

"Show me!"

I looked at Hannah and saw in her eyes a trace of that old mischievous glint. "Me too!" She laughed. "I'm in no way scandalized by a bit of bare behind."

I pulled down my jeans and showed them the mark on my bum. Tully stared at the strawberry mark, shaped like a heart, on my right flank. Then he dropped his ragged trousers and compared the two marks.

"They're identical!" Hannah cried, astonished and delighted.

"They are," said Tully.

"Yes." I zipped my jeans up.

Tully thought for a while and then he said, "If you haven't been kidding me with all that coming-from-the-future foolishness, then maybe it's true that I'm your great-grandfather. Perhaps you came back to save me from the sea and the soldiers so you could be born. Now, isn't that the conundrum for you!" He spat on his hands and rubbed them together. "But what if you had never saved me and I had died there on the strand, drowned, the life gone out of me?"

"But then Tom would never be born!" said Hannah.

"That's right," said Tully to his sister. "And if Tom was never born, then I would never be saved so he might be born!" He scratched his head, intrigued with the puzzle he'd set himself. "It's a grand idea, but it'd have the best thinkers in the world scratching their heads. And I don't believe it. Not a bit of it, even though we're alike as a pair of crows. I couldn't possibly be your ancient grandfather."

"No?"

"No." He shook his head. "You must think I'm a fool." He gave a harsh laugh. "You might just as well say it was the shee-og brought you here, for that would make far better sense."

"Perhaps they did," I said, thinking of the goblin gatekeeper.

"Oh, Tully!" Hannah said in disgust.

Tully stared at me. I could almost see the shee-og dancing about in his mind. "Twaddle!" he said finally. "Or crap, as you say, Tom. I think you made it all up."

Ma and Brendan were to be buried outside the city, in the countryside, in a pauper's grave, which was for people who had no money for a proper burial. There was a cart starting out from the workhouse early in the morning with the coffins—I counted eighteen plain wooden boxes, some of them little more than roughly nailed packing crates—and the mourners, only five including myself, Hannah, and Tully. When the cart and driver showed up in the yard the coffins were loaded by two workers. Tully lifted both coffins onto the back of the cart, not letting the driver or the workhouse staff touch them. Maggie's and Brendan's names had already been rough-carved into the lid, by a skilled carver by the look of it, but carelessly, like he was in a hurry: Maggie Theresa Monaghan; Brendan Thaddeus Monaghan, with the date, 1848. We sat in the cart beside the coffins.

The other two mourners were women burying their children. One was Mary, the other Patty. They were Irish. Each had lost a child to the famine fever, a seven-year-old girl and a four-year-old boy. They had little to say and, after a small polite exchange of information, sat in the cart in silence.

The morning was bright and fine with a cover of high patchy cloud and a sun that peeped through now and then; a keen wind blew up from the river in occasional cold gusts. The horse was a slow plodder but we were soon out of the city, heading eastward into the countryside on a well-worn road.

Tully sat with his head in his hands, elbows on knees; Hannah, with her back straight, eyes fixed unswervingly on the horizon. They didn't speak. Tully was wearing his mother's marriage ring, the one he had carved for her, on a black bootlace about his neck.

After a while I could see a small village with its church steeple glinting in the far distance and I watched it get larger and disappear as we dipped briefly into a dingle, then reappear as we crested the hill, this time with a good view of the church.

I stared.

"What's the name of this place?" I shouted up to the driver.

"Old Swan."

I knew it! I was looking at Snozzy's church, but not the Snozzy's I was familiar with, the one with worn sandstone blocks sooty black from a century and a quarter of smoky coal fires and its steeple pitted with shrapnel from Hitler's bombs. This church, the one I was looking at now, was newly built: its recently carved sandstone a rich red, its steeple rising new and shiny-like to the sky. I couldn't take my astonished eyes off it.

ST. OSWALD'S PARISH said the painted wooden sign at the lych-gate.

I had come full circle: I was back at Snozzy's.

Built, I remembered, six years before, in 1842.

I tore my eyes away from the church and looked about me. The village was small: a scattering of houses and shops, no Precky Road plugged and roaring with traffic, only a sign, PRESCOT LANE, with green hedges, a blacksmith's shop with a stable, a yard with horses, and an Old Swan Inn at the corner, where it still is today except it's not an inn, just an ordinary pub.

As we drew into the church grounds I could see several other carts piled high with coffins. A couple of men were unloading and stacking them near the piles of dirt. They wore work gloves and their mouths were covered with handkerchiefs against disease and the smell of death.

I jumped out of the cart and looked down into my mass grave, mine because I knew this place very well: it was my beginning place, my crossroads in time, my pit of destiny. I felt the pull of it at me.

The grave was big. Including a large area where many people were already buried, it measured like, what, fifteen feet wide? Twenty-five long? Down in its depths a gang of six men were digging, working furiously as though they couldn't dig fast enough to accommodate all the coffins being delivered, filling barrows with dirt for other men to wheel quickly up wooden ramps to ground level to empty them and nip back down for the next load. There were already many hundreds of coffins in the grave, stacked sixteen high at one end, leaving a space of a few feet for soil to cover the topmost ones.

We stood by and watched coffins being lowered into the pit, and when it came the turn for Ma and Brendan to go down, Tully knelt beside the pit and prayed. Mary and Patty fell to their knees beside him and sobbed quietly as the bodies of their children were put down into the ground. Hannah didn't kneel or pray, but stood stiff as a statue, her face and lips white. I couldn't pray either, though my heart was bursting.

And then I felt the grave pulling at me. Like a magnet.

It wanted me back.

I resisted the pull, backing away from the grave edge, but then I realized I had to return. It made sense; I had come full circle and whatever it was I had been sent to do had been done.

When all the coffins were in, the men paused in their digging and removed their cloth caps and wiped the sweat from their brows while a tired, gray-faced Snozzy's priest muttered a prayer and sprinkled holy water into the grave over the latest batch of coffins. The brief ceremony over, the men went back to work. I could have sworn I saw the gatekeeper among the workers, leaning on his staff and staring up at me, but then he was gone, lost in the toil and broil of bodies and coffins below. A shiver ran up my spine; he was waiting for me.

And the driver was waiting to return. Mary and Patty had decided to stay in the village. "There's nothing and no one waiting for us in the city," Mary said to the driver. "We're as well to stay here."

Patty said nothing; her face was swollen from the crying.

Tully jumped up onto the cart and reached out a hand for Hannah and hauled her aboard. I stayed where I was.

Tully said, "Are you not coming back with us, Tom?"

I shook my head. "Do you remember I told you about a big grave?"

"I do," said Tully.

I jerked my head in the direction of the pit. "This is it. This is the place I started out from." I looked about me. "This church, this . . . village. It's mine. I can get back home from here."

Tully regarded me solemnly. "Then it's goodbye?"

"Oh, Tom!" Hannah gave a cry and jumped down off the cart and threw herself on me. "Don't go! Please! Come with us!"

I shook my head. "It's not to be, Hannah."

She crushed me with surprising strength. There were tears in her eyes. I held her. Strands of her loose brown hair blew in my eyes. "I'll miss you, Hannah, you know that, don't you?"

She nodded, unable to speak.

"The first day I met you, there was a black smudge right here." I touched her nose.

She smiled through her tears.

The driver was starting to get impatient, tapping his whip on the side of the cart.

"I'll remember everything about you, Hannah. I won't ever forget you, I promise."

"And I'll never forget you, Tom. You will be with me all my life, till the day I die. Here . . ."

She slipped the Claddagh ring off her finger and pushed it onto mine. "Here's my promise. Keep it for me. See the hands about the heart? They're my hands. This way I'll always be holding you."

I helped her up onto the cart.

"God go with you, Tom," said Tully.

I looked up at him, shielding my eyes from the brightness. "And with you both. Will you still go to America?"

"I don't know. We might stay here. But we'll survive, thanks to you."

I studied his face. It wasn't the same sulky, childish face that had glowered at me from a dark corner of a stone cottage on Achill Island. This face was already harder and wiser, more culpable, more like my own. I grinned. "You'll be all right, Grandfather. Do you believe it yet?"

He smiled. "I believe that you believe it, Tom, and that's good enough for me." He dropped down off the cart and put his arms about me and held me without saying anything more. Then he leaped back onto the cart and waved a hand at me and the driver urged the horse away and Hannah was crying and that was the last I ever saw of the Monaghans.

25

. . . expecting to see ghosts

It was cold in the grave.

And smelly. After everyone had gone, when the church grounds were deserted and quiet and dark, with the grave pulling at me, with only the light from the moon, I walked down the ramp, the one used by the wheelbarrow men, lifted and wrestled the two Monaghan coffins down onto the grave bottom, then settled down on the cold hard clay beside them. I wasn't scared. They were family.

I waited.

Watching Hannah drive away had been hard; parting from her had been a terrible wrench, the hardest thing I ever did. But I knew I had to return and I was ready for it. The funny thing was I *wanted* to go back. Don't ask me why: I don't know, except since Brendan died I'd been thinking quite a bit about Brian, wondering if he was okay.

Like I said, I wasn't scared sitting in the bottom of the grave, well, not much, but it was hard to ignore the smell of death and disease all around me. I closed my eyes and waited, trying to concentrate on the twentieth-century churchyard, willing the boomerang effect to take me back, thinking about seeing Brian again, and about Hannah and Tully back in the city, just the two of them now.

Hannah was lost to me. I knew that. She was gone. I would never see her again. But I'll never forget her. Never. And I'll always miss her.

Losing people was too easy. I never knew my father, so I guess you could say he was lost. I lost my mother; then the Mullens; the Feinbergs next; now the Monaghans. Too easy.

I couldn't sleep because of the cold; I lay beside the coffins, shivering on the hard clay. Just when I'd almost given up and was thinking I couldn't stand the smell any longer the darkness turned to the now familiar green light, and there was the gate-keeper, a glimpse only, then the pains came and I knew I was back, stiffening with the shock of them, gritting my teeth and hanging on.

When the pains had gone I wiped the tears from my face and saw that all the piles of coffins were old. Maggie's and Brendan's, beside me, were unbroken, but the names carved on the lids were so blackened and rotted with age that I could barely make them out.

Hannah's ring was still on my finger, the bog oak seeming darker but the smudge in the heart grain still the color of butter. I ran a finger over its hard smoothness and felt Hannah's hands around my heart.

I looked up at a cloudy sky. I stood, but forgot my sprained ankle and stumbled. I felt it gingerly. The swelling had gone, but it felt stiff. No sign of old Harry O'Neill's cane. No sounds of machines or workers. No bad smell, just the sweet rich sniff of earth and mold and decay. Glad to be moving but carefully favoring the stiff ankle, I climbed up out of the pit, leaving the coffins where they were. I found the tools I'd be needing in an equipment shed near the crane, and left them for later. Then I crawled under the fence. I couldn't see a guard anywhere. I stood up and looked about me; I was back all right. Sounds of traffic on Snozzy Street and Precky Road, Snozzy's church, sooty and chipped and old, people dressed in their Sunday best pouring out the front doors after Sunday mass, the usual geezer in his shiny-at-the-elbows gray suit and cloth cap standing on the steps rattling his collection box at them with his usual monotonous "Peter's pence" chant. Made me feel like I was home. I'd never thought of Old Swan as home before.

Sunday. Just right.

It felt like September still, or October, but not March. The horse chestnuts inside the lych-gate were still shedding their leaves; conkers shone richly like promises in the grass.

I nipped—well, okay, limped, though I knew the ankle would be fine once the stiffness had gone—down Snozzy

Street, my first thought being to find Brian. Assuming he was still in Old Swan—did I mention that every district in Liverpool has a number? Old Swan is 13, wouldn't you know it—and hadn't been sent to Wavertree or Aigburth or Bootle or some other district, then he would be still at the Smileys' on Leinster.

Mrs. Smiley answered the door. She was a tall, thin old biddy with big gray hair. Brian was out, she said, probably in the park. She gave me a hard look. "You must be the Tommy Brian talks about all the time."

"Tom."

"Hmmmn." She looked me up and down, then closed the door.

Old cow.

Brian was kicking a ball about with a mob of kids and saw me coming and ran like a lunatic, leaping over the KEEP OFF THE GRASS sign, waving his arms, yelling, "Tom! It's Tom!" I thought he was going to throw his great arms around me and squeeze me like a toothpaste tube, or even kiss me, but I saved myself the embarrassment by fending him off, holding out an arm like a bobby on traffic duty outside Anfield Stadium.

But I was glad to see him.

So I told him.

I said, "I'm glad to see you, Brian."

His face collapsed. I thought he was going to cry.

The other kids weren't far behind, their eyes bugging out at the sight of me.

"Where you go?" Willy wanted to know.

"Where you go, Tom?" Brian echoed, dancing about like he needed to pee.

"You bleedin' son of a gun!" said Willy. "Everyone thought you ran off to London."

"Not London," I said. "I'll tell you about it sometime." I turned to Brian. "Right now I need your help, Bri. Come on." I said to the others, "See you guys later."

Brian followed me, mouth open and tongue hanging out, panting like a St. Bernard whose master was finally taking him for a walk after three weeks shut up inside. He couldn't turn off his happiness regulator; kept cavorting about like a drunken lunatic.

My ankle seemed to be working okay. We nicked a few things to eat, bread, some carrots, a packet of Scotch mints, as we walked along Precky Road, through Knotty Ash, then sat and ate them on top of the monkey ladder.

"Where you go, Tom?"

"I had to go away for a while, Bri."

"Same place you went the last time was it, Tom, same place?"

"That's right, Bri. I went into the past, back to 1848. People needed me."

Brian was silent for a while as he struggled with a thought. Then he said. "I need you, Tom."

"I know, Brian. I think maybe we need each other."

That made him happy again.

"What was the people's names, Tom?"

"The girl's name was Hannah. The boys were Tully and Brendan." I told Brian the story, keeping it simple; he listened in silence until I was finished and then he said, "That's a good story, Tom. I liked it. You tell good stories, Tom."

"Thanks, Brian."

That's all it was to Brian, a good story. I don't think he understood half of it anyway, but that was okay; telling it made me feel good.

"I'm glad you're back, Tom."

I looked at his big face that never told a lie.

"If you have to go away again will you take me with you, Tom?"

"Yes, Brian, we'll stay together, don't worry."

"We'll always stay together, right, Tom?"

"Yes. We'll always stay together."

"No matter what, right, Tom?"

"Right, Bri, no matter what."

"I'm glad you're back, Tom."

"How's your fozzy? They still making you do sums and stuff?"

"I wish you was there, Tom. Be different if you was there."

"Sums and reading is it?"

"I get everything wrong, Tom, everything. They make me do things over and over."

We'd munched all our stuff and there was nothing left, so I dropped down off the monkey ladder. We drank some water from the fountain and then played on the swings for a bit, and after that we joined in with a bunch of kids playing football, but I was worried about my ankle, so I stopped after a while and just watched. Then I sat with Brian on top of the monkey ladder again and afterward we lay in the grass and I fell asleep.

It was late when I woke. Brian had slept, too.

Time to check with the Two Peas to see if I was written off; gone missing; absent without leave. I'd been gone almost three weeks. They would have kicked me out by now. The SS, too. I could see and hear Nicebum give a little sigh as she ruled a perfect inked line through my name: ~~Tom Mullen~~.

Derby Lane, number 39. Brian hung back anxiously, well away from the door. The door was locked, so I knocked loud and hard. Percy was out. It took a long time for Paula to come to the door, hair in curlers, ciggy in her gob, eyes bugging out when she saw me.

"What do you want, you little snot? You don't live here no more."

"My stuff." I especially wanted my *Science Facts* and my calculator and magnifying glass.

"Your school uniform's gone to Family Placement, and your shoes; they paid for them, after all, but I threw out your other junk. Go search in the rubbish dump." She laughed and slammed the door in my face.

I could always get another *Science Facts*, but it was the Feinbergs who'd given me the calculator and the magnifying glass.

"Rotten old cow!"

"Rotten old cow!" Brian repeated happily.

I reminded him I needed his help.

He was chuffed that I needed him. "What do you want me to do, Tom?" Eager, like a puppy as usual.

"It's the grave. I'll tell you the rest when we get there, but you've got to promise to help no matter what."

His eyebrows collided. "I don't like that place."

"Do you promise to help?"

"I wanna help you, Tom, no matter what."

"You promise?"

"Okay, I promise."

He looped an arm round my shoulder and we traipsed up Snozzy Street knotted together like two pieces in a daisy chain, except we were no daisies. Then we uncoupled to duck under the fence when the guard wasn't looking and stood on the edge, looking down into the pit.

I could feel nothing, no magnet drawing me, no urge to let go.

He couldn't believe it when I told him what I wanted him to do. He started moaning.

"It'll be okay, Brian, trust me."

"But, Tom!"

"Listen to me. What do you think they're doing with all these coffins every day? What d'you think they're doing? Answer me that."

"I don't know, Tom."

"Carting them off and burning them to ashes, that's what. And nobody knows who these people were. It isn't right."

It was no good: he didn't understand.

"Could we go now, Tom?" he moaned. "It's getting dark."

"You promised to help, Bri."

"That's right, Tom." He looked about nervously. "I promised."

I took the three lengths of rope I'd found earlier in the day from the equipment shed, climbed down into the grave, and tied two of the ropes to Brendan's coffin, checking to make sure the knots wouldn't slip. Brian caught the rope ends I threw up to him. Then I tied the third rope around the middle of the coffin to hold it off the earth wall while Brian started drawing it easily to the top.

We did the same with Maggie's coffin. By the time both coffins was safely on the top it was a bit hard to see in the lowering darkness, but I showed Brian the place where the names had been carved, tracing the letters—many missing because they'd rotted away—with a finger and spelling them out.

I knew Brian wouldn't understand, but I had to say it. "This is Brendan, one of the boys I told you about."

"This is Brendan," Brian repeated.

"That's right," I said. "And this is his mother. They need our help."

"Need our help."

We pushed the coffins and the shovels and ropes under the fence, the hardest part, then carried everything round the side of the church into the nuns' burial ground, where all the graves are marked with little iron Celtic crosses with names on them: Sister Celia Marie, 1887–1947; Sister Agnes, 1865–1939; and so on, all the dead Sisters of Mercy who'd taught in the Infants'

School. There's dozens of them, little grassy plots with crosses, in rows stretching the length of the private garden behind the church presbytery, the perfect place for Maggie and Brendan.

We put the coffins down on the grass. Brian complained of the cold and dark, looking over his shoulder like he was expecting to see ghosts any minute. I had chosen a place out of sight to anyone standing near the church. There are wild fuchsia bushes against the presbytery wall near the last row of crosses, though I couldn't see them so well in the dark. "Dig here," I said, pointing to a spot up against the wall and between two clumps of fuchsia.

It was quiet in the nuns' garden, not even the noise of traffic. That's what it's like, a garden, grass and flowers—dahlias, I think, and wild crimson fuchsias like the ones in Achill—and rows of iron crosses, each about a foot high. We dug down, Brian powerfully with all the strength of his big arms and shoulders. The owl hooted from the steeple and we stopped digging for a minute, scared, pulling ourselves together before bending again to the task.

It took longer than I thought and I was tired. "That should be deep enough," I said.

We lowered the coffins carefully into what I hoped would be their final resting place.

"They'll be safe here."

"Safe here," Brian repeated.

We shoveled the dirt over them, and trampled it down, and tidied the place up the best we could in the darkness, hoping the fresh dig wouldn't be noticed. Then on the way out we tossed the shovels and the ropes over the fence and scarpered out of there as fast as we could go.

"Thanks, Brian," I said. It was very dark. He wanted me to walk home with him, so I did.

The Smileys came to the door, both of them, and gave us hard looks when they saw our filthy clothes. Mr. Smiley was a big guy, red-faced and stern. Retired couple, very old. Bent on teaching Brian to read and write and do sums. Barking mad, both of them.

. . . moment of truth

I stayed the night at Child Services, round the back of the Juvy, in a crowded dormitory. They knew me: I'd been there plenty of times before.

I nipped over to the mass grave site the next morning, ducking under the fence so I could borrow a shovel and take a look at the work going on. A bulldozer was already reshaping one part of the site for the foundation of the new school as the last of the coffins were being lifted out.

I watched. The crane lowered a slingful of coffins into the back of a truck. A man released the sling and stood back while the crane raised the empty sling and the coffins tumbled together in a pile. When the truck was full it left the site, rumbling away down Montague Street.

I grabbed a shovel. One of the workmen yelled at me. I gave him the finger and ducked back out, heading over to the nuns' burial ground, where I did a little more tidying. When it was finished I planted a few small wild fuchsia cuttings on the grave in the hope that one of them would take. I stood back and admired the grave, happy that Maggie and Brendan Monaghan had not been carted off and tossed into an incinerator like they were rubbish. Maybe one day I could place a stone on the grave, a proper stone with their names and the name of the father on it and Hannah's and Tully's names, too. I knew what I'd write: Died 1848: Maggie Theresa Monaghan, loving wife of Thaddeus; also their son Brendan Thaddeus Monaghan, 17, brother of Tully and Hannah. R.I.P. Or something like that.

I sat on the grass, my back against the wall. It was quiet in the garden, no traffic noises, only the sound of the wind tumbling autumn leaves and Hannah humming an Irish song to herself.

I smiled at her. "You're always singing."

She stretched up her arms and fixed fuchsias in her hair.

I watched her.

"Have I them on right, Tom?"

"I'll miss you, Hannah."

I don't know how long I sat in the garden beside the grave. Then I took the shovel back.

———

I wasn't quite ready to go back to school yet. So I wandered over to the SS.

Nicebum seemed happy to see me. "Tom Mullen! Child Services told me you were back. I thought you'd run off to New York!"

"Or Robin Hood's Bay? The name's Tom Monaghan now. I changed it."

Just as I said that, I felt something odd, something sudden and important, a click of recognition, like my wobbling mollies had righted themselves once and for all. There was a certainty to it, a moment of truth, you might say, like my life had changed and there was no going back and nothing from now on would ever be quite the same. It was a good feeling.

Nicebum smiled. "Where did you run off to, Tom *Monaghan*?"

"I've been right here in Liverpool, but I visited the nineteenth century, 1847 to be exact."

"It must have been exciting."

"And 1848."

"Fascinating."

"It was."

Nicebum riffled through my file. "It just won't do, the running away, I mean. You must promise not to do it again. If there are problems, you must come to me."

I weighed her up as she sat behind her desk. She looked crisp, as usual, clean, shining brown hair, silk shirt—cream-color, with a dainty little bow at the neck—lipstick a nice pale pinkish color.

"I have bad news and good news, Tom. I'll tell you the bad first. The bad news is I can't put you back with the Partridges."

"That's good."

"Really? Mrs. Partridge seemed so nice, bringing in your uniform, all nicely washed and pressed, and your schoolbooks, saying how sorry she was to lose you, even if you both didn't always see eye to eye. The poor woman was almost crying."

"I bet!"

"Well, the other good news is you have a choice. First, my application to transfer you to another district went through all right, and now there's a nice place in Fairfield that just became available, with the loveliest couple. A day either way and you would have lost it." She flashed me a dazzling smile. "You would have a room all to yourself; there's already one boy there, twelve years old and he loves it; there'd be only the two of you. You would go to St. Sebastian's. Doesn't that sound wonderful?"

It did sound wonderful. I had been to Snebby's before; it was okay.

"Second choice is, I had a call this morning from Mrs. Smiley. She would like to take you. They've got Brian, as you know. They didn't want a second child. But they like you, Tom. And Brian never stops talking about you. So they asked for you. Would you like to live with the Smileys?"

I didn't like the Smileys much; a cold pair of lunatics, I'd guessed, but they probably meant well, trying to teach Brian stuff, and I'd met a lot worse.

"You would have to share a room with Brian, of course."

With Brian.

"But you wouldn't need to change schools."

Fairfield was a good mile away from Old Swan. Liverpool District number 6. Brian could never find his way there.

"The choice is yours, Tom. It's not often we can offer a choice, as you know, especially with all the new funding cuts to the program."

I knew what I wanted.

Nicebum said, "They're not New York, or Robin Hood's Bay, I know, but . . ."

"The Smileys' is fine."

I'd lost enough people; I didn't want to lose Brian. I wasn't really a loner after all; maybe nobody is.

Nicebum looked at me in silence for several beats, like she was surprised and was trying to figure me out. Then she smiled, made a notation in the file, and tossed it into the basket marked FOR FILING.

The place looked better organized: no messy stacks of files, surfaces clean and tidy. Nicebum was a hard worker.

I got up to go. "Remember to change my name in your book. It's Monaghan, spelled . . ."

She laughed. "I know how to spell it, Tom."

On the way over to my new fozzy I did a little shopping, just one item. Didn't nick it: paid for it with the last few coins in my pocket.

I probably mentioned it already, but number 19 Leinster

Road, like most of the older houses in Liverpool, is an ordinary red brick terrace house. The Smileys have it all to themselves. Except for Brian, of course.

I gave the brass knocker a loud hammering thump just to let them see I wasn't going to take any crap from anyone. Mrs. Smiley came hard-faced to the door and said, "No need to break the door down. Wipe your feet and come in." I ignored the mat and followed her into the living room. "You already met my husband," she said. "Ted, this is Tommy Mullen, hasn't any things."

"Tom Monaghan," I said.

She stared at me. "The young lady said—"

"Tom Monaghan," I said again.

Mr. Smiley didn't get up from his easy chair where he was reading his newspaper but gave me a curt nod. "You got no things?"

"No."

"How come?"

"Last fozzy threw them out."

He stared at me for a while and I stared back. "You're welcome here, boy," he said, "so long as you follow a few simple rules, you understand?"

I nodded. "What about Brian?"

"What about him?"

"How's he doing with the sums and stuff?"

Smiley put down his newspaper and shook his head, worried. "Progress is slow."

"You might say very, very slow," said the missus, also shaking her head.

"The boy is stubborn as a mule," said Smiley.

"Come upstairs," said the missus, "and I'll show you your room."

I followed her up the stairs. On the landing she said, "This is the bathroom." We climbed four more steps to the first closed door. "This is Mr. Smiley's room." At the second closed door she said, "And this is my room." She stopped and turned to me. "On no account are you to go into my room or Mr. Smiley's room." At the third closed door she said, "This is yours and Brian's room." She threw the door open. I looked in. Tiny room, one bed, chest of drawers. The usual.

"We'll have to find a bed for you," said Mrs. Smiley. "The chest you can share."

We went back downstairs and I sat at the kitchen table while the missus made a pot of tea. Smiley was still reading his newspaper.

When Brian got home from school and saw me sitting at the kitchen table with the Smileys, drinking tea and eating an arrowroot bicky, he was so chuffed he couldn't stop grinning. Then when the missus told him I was staying there for good his eyebrows zoomed all over his face. Laughing and shouting, he grabbed me and bounced me around and near broke my sodding back and squeezed the life out of me. Mr. Smiley had to make him let me go.

"Calm down, boy, calm down!" he yelled.

"I knew we'd be together again, Tom!" Brian cried. "I prayed hard every night. 'God,' I said, 'let me be back with Tom, same as before.' "

"Sit down, Brian," said the missus, "and have a cup of tea to calm your nerves."

Brian sat, his legs and feet still bouncing under the table.

I reached into my pocket. "Here," I said, handing him a crushed Kit Kat. "I brought you a chocky-bicky."

...world full of monaghans

October, Monday morning, and the school yard full of yellow leaves. I seemed to be noticing things more: trees and leaves and colors, stuff like that. Autumn colors, vivid and sharp. Were they always like that?

Me and Brian and a few of the other kids were waiting for the bell to go. I watched the workmen on the building site of the new school. Brian went off to his special class where they were having a birthday party for one of the other kids and he didn't want to be late and miss anything.

The high corrugated fencing had disappeared from around the building site and the mass grave was history. Now all you could see were the concrete footings for the new building.

"It's funny there wasn't nothing in the papers about the grave," said Willy.

"Are you sure? Nothing in the *Echo*?"

"None of the papers."

"How do you know?"

Willy bit his nails. "Old Harry O'Neill reads all the papers and he says there was nothing. He looked for it, deliberate like."

"How is he then?" I made a mental promise to go see Mr. O'Neill and tell him I'd lost his cane.

"Looks okay, the old geezer."

We stood silently, watching the work. I thought about the grave and its hundreds of coffins, all gone now, burnt to ashes; soon the new school building would cover the place. I thought about Maggie and Brendan, safe in the nuns' garden.

The bell rang and we moved reluctantly into school under the watchful eye of Miss Hewitson.

I reckoned that Tully never got to America, that he stayed in Liverpool. Which explained why I was here and not in New York.

Or Robin Hood's Bay.

Football practice. Late afternoon and a chill wind. I was in my football shorts and jersey.

Coach Greensleeves in his shorts, too, Coach Lanny sharp as usual in his tracksuit, lanyard, and whistle.

Lanny signaled for me to drop out. I followed him to the

clubhouse. Greensleeves tagged along. Lanny was cheesed off. He glared at me. "You already missed seven practices, Mullen. The ankle's no excuse; you could've done upper-body workout. Give me one good reason why we should keep you on the team."

"There was no way I could make it, Coach. Honest. I had to go away. I couldn't help it. And it's not Mullen anymore. I changed my name to Monaghan."

Lanny shot Greensleeves a look and gave a laugh. "What, you adopt the kid, Jamie, or what?"

I didn't understand what he meant but I said nothing.

Greensleeves said, "Look, Lanny, the kid had a bad sprain on that ankle. We could give him a break."

Lanny shrugged. "You're the boss. You want to give him a break, then we'll give him a break." He looked at me. "How's the ankle?"

"Still a bit stiff."

Greensleeves said, "You better just take it easy for a while, Tom, till it's stronger."

Greensleeves made me do some stretches and then we took a seat together on the bench and watched the team working out with Lanny, Greensleeves shouting occasional instructions from the bench. I folded my arms across my chest and hunched my shoulders against the cold. I could see Brian over in the clubhouse thumping the pop machine. Greensleeves zipped up his jacket.

Brian trundled over and sat beside us with his pop. "You not playing, Tom?"

"Not today, Bri."

Greensleeves went to his truck in the parking lot and came back wearing his bomber jacket. He threw me a sweater. "Thanks, Coach." I pulled it on over my head.

"No sense in freezing."

"What did Lanny mean about adopting me?" I asked Greensleeves. "He being funny?"

Greensleeves shook his head. "I thought maybe it was you was the one being funny, Tom. Why the name change to Monaghan?"

"It's a long story, Coach."

"Because my name is Monaghan, as you very well know."

"*Your* name Monaghan? I thought your name was Greensleeves, Jamie Greensleeves, same as on your truck. Everyone calls you Greensleeves."

"Maybe they do, but my real name is Monaghan. Says so on the truck. Greensleeves is the business name."

I thought for a minute and remembered the name, J. MONAGHAN, in tiny print, low down on the side of the doors, next to the truck's weight. How could I have forgotten that? I shrugged; Monaghan was a fairly common name.

We watched the practice.

World full of Monaghans. Like Smiths and Joneses.

Greensleeves said, "What you got there on your finger?"

I showed him my ring. Did I mention how the bog oak is a darker color since I got back? Except for the grain in the heart.

His eyes narrowed. "Take it off and let me see."

I eased the ring off and handed it to him.

"Where did you get this ring, Tom?"

"That's another long story. And you wouldn't believe it anyway."

I watched him reach in over his top shirt button and pull out his gold chain, and I felt my heart give a lurch of joy, as I now knew for sure that Tully had survived back in 1848, that he'd beaten the poverty and disease. And if Tully had made it, then Hannah must have made it, too. How could I know? Greensleeves' chain ran through a familiar ring. My eyes bugged as I watched him undo the clasp and slide the ring off the chain. He handed it to me without a word. Greensleeves' ring, with its heart, hands, and crown, wasn't made of brass or silver or gold or stone; instead it was carved from bog oak, like mine. It was, without any doubt, Tully's ring; I'd have known it anywhere. I ran my thumb over the smudge in its heart while my own heart thumped like I'd just sprinted twice around the practice field.

We handed the rings back in silence, the air about us charged with words unsaid.

Greensleeves looked at me through narrowed eyes, saying nothing, waiting for me to speak.

I held up Hannah's ring. "I saw Tully Monaghan carve this ring." I pushed it back on my finger. "He made it for his sister. Her name is—was—Hannah. Hannah gave it to me."

Greensleeves put his ring back on the chain.

I already knew the answer, but Greensleeves could've picked the ring up in a pawnshop or some other place, so I asked anyway. "Where did you get your ring, Coach?"

He narrowed his eyes again and looked at me long and hard. Then he said in a funny voice, "It belonged to my father." He continued watching me.

When I said nothing he said, "Maybe you better tell me that long story of yours, Tom, okay? Tell me why you changed your name to Monaghan."

28
. . . a mother knows

So I did. I told Greensleeves why I changed my name to Monaghan.

And that's about it; that's my story.

The rest is history, as they say.

Old Swan isn't so bleak anymore. Maybe it never was; maybe I was the bleak one. Anyway, I can live with it: life is too short to worry about stuff. The Smileys are not very smiley; they're not likely to be voted the mellowest people in Liverpool, but the food isn't too bad. On a scale of one to ten, ten being the highest, I'd rate them like, what, an eight? Which is a major improvement on the Two Peas.

Anyway, it's temporary.

I like that word. Temporary. Everything is temporary if you think about it.

I've stopped nicking stuff; there's no need. Besides, I can't forget what Tully said about an honest man being the noblest work of God. His dad, Thaddy Monaghan, told him that. So I try to stay honest. I don't let Brian nick stuff either.

Greensleeves is my dad, of course. And you don't think life is crazy?

We figured it out. Greenslee—I'd better start calling him Dad, or Jamie—Jamie's dad got his ring off his dad, who got it off Tully. Anyway, Jamie's mum and dad are still alive. His dad's name is Jack and his mother's name is Ann and they live in Old Swan, too. So I've got grandparents. Grandfather Jack looks a bit like me and Tully—in old snapshots—but not much. Jack's dad was James, and James' dad was Tully. Also known as great-great-grandfather Tully from Achill.

Immediately after practice—the day we'd compared the rings—Jamie took me and Brian home in his van. He drove fast. Hardly spoke a word the whole way. Just said he wanted me to meet someone.

It was getting dark by the time we got there. Big old ramshackle house next to the Greensleeves Garden Centre in Thomas Lane.

Greensl—Jamie introduced us to his missus, Alice, a tall woman, slim and neat, with dark hair going gray, greenish eyes, with a nice quiet way about her. She made us tea and brought out a big plate of Cadbury's milk chocolate biscuits and we all sat down, me and Brian on either end of a long sofa with enough room in the middle for a whole football team, Jamie and the missus in easy chairs, all facing each other like it was a TV discussion group.

I mentioned that the missus has a quiet way about her, but right then she seemed agitated, and so was I if you really want to know the truth, I mean, how would you feel if you finally got to meet . . . anyway, my insides felt emptier than a fozzy fridge.

Jamie asked me to tell my story again, but this time in full. Leaving nothing out. "I want Alice to hear this," he said.

So I told the whole story. Brian was silent except for his biscuit chewing, which sounded like a beaver chomping on an elm tree. I told about the mass grave the builders discovered under Snozzy's school yard, and then I described Achill, the starving people, Thaddy being shot, Maggie dying of the famine fever, then Brendan dying, and all the rest of it, but leaving out stuff like the Champion of Mayo.

I paused for a minute while Alice fetched the whole tin of Cadbury's and told Brian to just help himself.

Then I described the burial of hundreds of famine and fever victims in the mass grave when Snozzy's church was only six years old, and the priest saying prayers over the coffins. I told how Hannah gave me her ring before we parted.

Alice looked at the ring. Then she looked at Jamie's, which he took off his neck chain. Then she looked at mine again.

I finished off by telling about the family grave that me and Brian made in the nuns' garden.

By this time Brian had demolished the whole tin of biscuits

and was looking toward the kitchen wondering if there were any more.

Jamie asked me a bunch of questions.

Then his missus asked me a bunch of questions, mainly about my age and background ("Subject's History"), including the fozzies I was in when I was little. She kept dabbing at her eyes with a handkerchief, especially when I mentioned Toys.

Jamie gave her a look.

She got up and sat on the sofa beside me and took my hand and said she was my mother.

Said she knew as soon as I walked in through the door. How could she know? A mother knows, she said.

Heart thumping, I asked her how come she left me in Toys, in Lewis's department store.

She said she didn't leave me in Toys.

Turns out it wasn't my mother who left me in Toys when I was about a year old, it was someone else.

I had been kidnapped.

It was in all the papers, Jamie said.

So the woman who left me in Toys was probably the same one who kidnapped me out of my pram from outside Kwik Save in Old Swan when I was only a month old, the same one who kept me for almost a year and then left me downtown in Toys for someone else to take care of. That's what we think happened, though we'll never know for sure.

Alice wondered why Social Services didn't tie it all together—the child found in the department store and the baby stolen a year before.

"Tie it all together? You must be joking!" I said. "The SS have trouble tying their shoelaces!"

Greensleeves said, "And it's a big city, Alice. Kids get abandoned almost every day."

Anyway, my real mother, Alice Monaghan, gave me up for lost, never thinking she'd ever see me again. She keeps hugging me. Says she can't believe I'm real.

And my proper birthday is December 19, just a few days after the guessed one. I don't like my real name, Jason. Too posh. Besides, Hannah wouldn't like it if I changed. So I'm keeping Tom. My mother has thought of me for thirteen and three-quarter years as Jason, but she's getting used to calling me Tom. "It's a good name," she said.

So it never was my mother riding down in Lewis's elevator and running down Renshaw Street with her coat flapping after all. It was some poor crazy woman who needed a baby, so stole one and called him Tommy, and then decided she didn't need him anymore, or couldn't keep him, or had to lighten her load because she was sinking, or whatever.

So that's it. Alice Monaghan is my mother.

She works with Jamie in the plant-growing business.

She hugs me in front of everyone.

Which is downright embarrassing.

Or she squeezes my hand. And she asks more questions about all the places I lived and stuff like that, like she's trying to fill up thirteen and three-quarter years of empty spaces.

They want me to live with them, of course. They don't have any other kids. I told them I couldn't live with them because I wanted to stay with Brian. I explained that we couldn't be split up. We were best mates.

Jamie and Alice looked at Brian. Then they looked at each other. Then they looked at me. There was plenty of room for Brian, too, Alice said, and Jamie smiled and nodded.

So me and Brian haven't split up; we're still at the Smileys'. But as soon as the SS sorts it all out—don't hold your breath— we'll be living at Greensleeves' in Thomas Lane.

Like I said at the beginning, it all started when I fell into the grave. It finished when I found out who I am. So that's it. That's the story.

author's note

The Irish Famine really happened.

The mass grave in my story is true also.

The discovery of the grave in the grounds of St. Oswald's, Old Swan, Liverpool, took place in the autumn of 1973 when a contractor was instructed to relocate six or seven unidentified graves before excavations began for a new school building. The remains were carefully removed, but the contractor kept finding more and more coffins. A fence was erected to keep the curious out while explorations continued. The "six or seven graves" turned out to be a mass grave with 3,561 coffins in it. They were stacked sixteen high. Building could not begin until they had all been removed. The British Home Office gave orders for the remains to be incinerated. Construction of the new St. Oswald's school was delayed while the removal and incineration of the coffins and their contents was carried out in secrecy over the next eighteen months.

The discovery of the mass grave and the incineration of its coffins was hushed up for eight years, until September 6, 1981, when it was made the subject of an article in *The Catholic Pictorial.* Because of the secrecy and haste (for which I can discover no explanation) to incinerate the remains, nobody knows who, when, what, or why 3,561 people were buried together in a mass grave. St. Oswald's church claims to have no record of the burial. As far as I know, no record was kept of any names on any of the coffins before they were incinerated.

Cecil Woodham-Smith, in *The Great Hunger: Ireland 1845–1849* (Hamish Hamilton, 1962), describes how, during the first five months of 1847, 350,000 destitute and starving Irish landed in Liverpool, a city with a native population of 250,000. A fever epidemic of "enormous proportions" broke out. Many immigrants died of typhus (sometimes known as the Irish famine fever), or of relapsing fever, dysentery, diarrhea, or scurvy, and, because of the fear of contamination, had to be buried quickly in paupers' graves.

There are undoubtedly many other mass graves yet undiscovered, not only in Liverpool but also in other cities, like London, Glasgow, and Cardiff.

When I visited St. Oswald's in March the clergy were un-available for interview.

The British government Home Office has not answered my inquiries. A newspaper article reported that the H.O. has no record of a mass grave at St. Oswald's.

J.H. 1999